The Lady Bortei
Queen of Atlan

Inge Blanton

iUniverse LLC
Bloomington

THE LADY BORTEI
Queen of Atlan

iUniverse books may be ordered through booksellers or by contacting:

iUniverse LLC
1663 Liberty Drive
Bloomington, IN 47403
www.iuniverse.com
1-800-Authors (1-800-288-4677)

ISBN: 978-1-4917-2033-2 (sc)
ISBN: 978-1-4917-2034-9 (e)

Printed in the United States of America.

iUniverse rev. date: 06/05/2014

Alma woke up not knowing where she was. It was frightening. She had walked out of her house after an altercation with her husband, Sep, vowing never to return. What has happen to her?

Other books from Inge Blanton are:

A Place Called Nunnery

The story is not about Nuns, but about Naomi Atossa, about her survival and courage in the face of nearly overwhelming adversity.

Lost in Time

The story about a woman swept up in a Time-warp. She is thrown so far back in time she can find no identifiable landmarks. But she meets fascinating people through a series of remarkable adventures.

The Antarean Odyssey

The Antarean Odyssey is the birth of a people, their involvement with other worlds and the fiery end of their home world. The Odyssey covers eight books.

Book One

The Labors of Jonathan

At a party one evening, Jonathan Wright unintentionally eavesdrops on a conversation concerning a worldwide cartel, an interstellar trade agreement and aliens called

Altruscans, not imagining the peril his discovery and curiosity would lead him into.

Book Two

The Original Four

Sabrina, Ayhlean, Sarah and Kamila are the beginning of the Antarean people.

Book Three

Loss of Eden

The ending of childhood might compare to the loss of Eden. It is time for the Original Four to meet the world.

Book Four

Starship Trefayne

If Sargon aka Jim Thalon thought to have Sabrina safely on the Trefayne, he will soon learn otherwise.

Book Five

Misalliance

To fulfill a Planetary Alliance requirement, Commander Sarah Thalon, Chief Medical Officer of the Antares, becomes an intern on the planet Madras.

Book Six

Assignment Earth

Sabrina's assignment is to see whether Earth is ready to join the Planetary Alliance.

Book Seven

Matched

Sabrina finally finds a mate who is her match in almost everything and is daunted neither by her independence, nor her stubbornness.

Book Eight

I, Sargon

This is the history of Sargon aka Jim Thalon.

The Lady Bortei

Queen of Atlan

A story by Inge Blanton

CHAPTER ONE

Alma was finished preparing the evening meal. She was still standing at the stove when Sep, her husband, staggered in, his shirt front torn, drunk again. For Alma, it was the norm since his release from prison. First the drinking and now gambling. The judge had sentenced him to six years for beating a young boy nearly to death. Sep had had a bad temper . . . . always. She tried not to frown at him when he stood there in the kitchen.

Alma imagined a younger Sep whose emotions hadn't been quite as extreme. Most of his energy had gone into the challenge of building up the estate he had inherited from his father, and the dowry Alma had brought into the marriage had helped. They had three children, now grown, who had recently come back to help her with the estate, then left before their father could return.

The trouble with Sep, Alma had decided, was that when things went wrong, he took it personally. When the crop failed, it was because God and nature had conspired against him, nothing to do with planting the wrong crop into the wrong soil. After the first crop failure, they had borrowed money. The next two years had also been disasters. There had been no way to pay back the loan, so now they were sliding further into debt.

Sep's aberrant behavior had started with little things, first staying out late at the pub because he felt ignored when she was busy with the babies. Then, the first time he came home drunk, he had cornered her in the barn and tried to rape her. A fishing net, hung up to dry, served as a weapon that she slung over his head, using it to tie him down. Then she nearly beat him senseless with a rubber hose. For more than a week he had walked around meekly, but only because he was sore. The drinking diminished for a while, and he tried to stay at home.

However, at the pub, those six years ago, where he had sought an hour or two of solace, turned sour when taunts about his financial failures stirred up the bitterness in him. That was when he began taking out his frustrations on whoever was unlucky enough to get in his way. Now he was back and vindictive. During his six-year absence, Alma and the children had been successful in a second go with the estate.

"Do you want to eat?" Alma asked him, scarcely able to contain her loathing.

"Eat your slop!" His slurred shriek rose as spittle drooled down his chin.

She backed away from the stove as he came toward her.

Sniggering, he crooned, "Ah, scared of me, good, good, very good. I have news for you, my sweet. I have lost the whole dammed estate to Berty. The whole kit and caboodle," he blubbered, swinging his arm in a circle. "He cheated, that scum. I know he cheated. I just couldn't catch him at it. Everything's gone. All you have worked so hard for. Gone. I lost it all." There was pure malice in his face as he leered at her with red rimmed eyes. Shaking his fist, he staggered toward her. "This all comes from trying to show me up. You made me look like a fool. It's all your fault."

Suddenly, he grabbed the steaming pot off the stove and slung its contents across the room, splattering the walls and floor and spitting onto the front of her blouse and skirt.

Swinging the heavy pot sent him off balance. He dropped it, and as he stumbled toward her, she scooped up the pot and pressed the hot base against his protruding belly. He screamed and lunged at her. She swung the pot and hit him over the head with it. He fell hard and heavy. She looked down at him and felt no remorse as he laid groaning and rolling on the floor, trying to get up. Then he must have passed out. She checked him to make sure that he was still breathing.

It took a while for all of it to sink in. Overcome by anger and despair, she sat down on a chair, growing numb. She was so tired, and she felt so old. It took all her effort to pull herself up from the chair and go to the phone. She called Bert Hoover. He confirmed what Sep had told her in his drunken outburst.

"Alma," Bert added, "I wouldn't mind if you stayed on, but not Sep. He would only do more damage to the place. I'll give you enough time to move your things out. Sorry."

She made a sound as if to cry, then slowly set the phone in its cradle. She turned to look at the mess and shuddered. She left the kitchen, closing the door firmly behind her. In the hallway, she reached for her coat and scarf. Last week, the weather had turned colder, and today it was snowing for the first time, thick and heavy. The lawn and pastures were already covered. Locking the front door, not certain why that mattered, she walked down the path and out onto the highway. She was leaving, and the only thing she was sure of, there was no turning back. Ahead, there was the curtain of thick, white flakes. She looked up and flakes assaulted her face in cold, wet blobs, and then they suddenly stopped . . . .

***

Alma snapped awake. Her heart was pounding. She struggled to push back what covered her, warding off hands that weren't there. She felt alien, disconnected from her body. To awaken and not know where she was terrified her.

Closing her eyes, she reached deep within herself, reaching for an inner calm. She tried to remember what had happened to her and shuddered. There had been large, black eyes like limpid pools, deep and bottomless. Also, voices rustling like dry leaves.

There was an awful taste in her mouth.

She sneezed, then brushed an object from her face. It felt soft. She turned slowly onto her back. A glimmer of light shone from above. Dawn or evening, she thought. She squinted, thinking the light seemed to be from what looked like an airshaft. Her right hand absently moved over her covering. Fur? Fur was expensive. Who had money to buy expensive furs? She flung the cover back, and in shock, hurriedly retrieved it.

"Oh, my god, I always thought hell was hot, but this is freezing cold," she mumbled to herself. So, I must still be alive, she thought, her mouth in an ironic twist. After walking out of her house she knew she would have preferred to freeze to death than return home. She must have found shelter.

She raised her head and looked around. What she saw looked like a cell, small with a vaulted ceiling and a stone floor. Touching the stonewall . . . it was like ice. Warmth had never touched it. Where in the hell was she? She moved the fur aside and found she was lying on a stone slab. Not very comfortable; she preferred it soft. I must be having a nightmare she finally decided and went to lie back down.

***

Her second time awakening was less frightening, but not less confusing. The creaking of a door had awakened her. When she poked her nose out from under the furs she watched as a cowled figure with a steaming bowl came toward her.

Maybe I found my way to a monastery, she thought.

Slowly she sat up, making sure the fur covered every inch of her body. Again she paused, puzzled. Lifting the cover, she discovered she was now in her birthday suit. That's odd, she thought, I never sleep without nightclothes.

There was a grunt from her visitor, reminding her of his presence. When she looked up, he was proffering the bowl.

She took it after fixing the covers around her. The food was hot and spicy, some kind of stew. It tasted good. She ate quickly. When she handed the bowl back, she asked, "Would you please tell me where I am?"

A grunt was the only reply.

"You're not very talkative are you? Have you taken a vow of silence?" she asked, piqued.

Turning, he left as silently as he had come.

Her situation was getting to be absurd, but she knew she was not dreaming. How did I get here? Or better, who brought me here? She wished she knew how or why. She wanted to explore where she was, but it was too cold even to think of moving from under the fur. There was nothing more to do than wait to see how things developed.

Years ago, a priest had taught her how to meditate. Wrapping herself tightly inside the fur, she let herself drift. Suddenly, pictures flitted past her consciousness, like watching a screen. She remembered queer-looking creatures bending over her, their voices rustling. Another time, she was floating in warm water. Her disjointed thoughts and her lassitude and her constant sleepiness bothered her. She was concerned she might be on tranquilizers. She remembered someone speaking to her. "We will meet in the end. Be calm and look within." But she couldn't concentrate on anything else the voice had said. Suddenly, it was gone. She had fallen asleep.

***

Alma sat up, blinking in the faint light that came through curtains. She was in a curtained bed? She reached out and shoved one of the panels aside. This was a different place. Astonished, she look around at the unfamiliar surroundings. All the furniture resembled museum pieces. There was no fur, no vaulted ceiling; no icy wall! Have I been good and been released from the dungeon?

At least she had retained what Sep used to call her skewed sense of humor. His name was Sephrim, but everybody called him Sep. As she thought of him, an irritated expression crossed her face. At one time she had loved him, but not anymore. Then, he wasn't in this funny dream with her. She still had no idea what had happened since walking from her house into the snow. Maybe it didn't matter what was happening to her; she could already . . . she choked that thought. No, I'm not dead. Let's see where it goes from here.

There was a slight cough and someone pulled the other half of the curtain aside. Alma sat up straight.

"Good morning, my Lady. I see you are awake. I am Tan Rue," a robed figure introduced himself.

"And I'm in Camelot," Alma finished.

A raised eyebrow was all the answer she received.

"Never mind," Alma told him, and waved her arm. Her arm was in a sleeve? Looking down, she saw she wore a white nightgown that covered her from throat to toe. When did I put this on? she wondered.

"Would you like to leave your bed?" she was asked.

"Of course," she answered and quickly slid off the bed. As soon as her feet touched the floor, she collapsed. Astonishment registered in her face as her feet went out from under her. Appalled, she looked up at him. "There is more to this nightmare than I thought."

"My Lady, may I help you up?" Tan Rue asked solicitously, barely able to suppress a smile at her consternation.

"Don't you, my Lady me!" she told him irascibly. "My name is Alma." Her name was all she had to hold onto in this strange dream where she couldn't discern what was truth or deception. Or was it all real?

The door opened and another cowled figure came in with a tray of food. Tan Rue led her to a table and gently let her slide into the chair. "It will be a while before the weakness goes away," he told her.

"I had a fairly well-conditioned body before I left home. Now, please explain why I'm feeling this way?"

She had practiced yoga, and hard work had kept her body in good condition. Also, she was trained in martial arts. Her father had insisted on it. This was simply ridiculous, and she let him know it in no uncertain terms.

But he only listen patiently, then handed her a glass containing a gold liquid before serving her breakfast. She ate ravenously.

Having finished eating, she pushed the plate back. Folding her hands in front of her she looked at Tan Rue. "Now, if you would be so kind and tell me where I am and how I got here?"

"I'm . . ." He was interrupted by the door opening as an elderly Monk came in.

"Ah, I see our Lady is awake. How are you feeling?" he asked, solicitously.

"Feeling . . . how do you expect me to feel?"

Ignoring her, he asked Tan Rue. "Is she fit?"

"No, Master, she is still very weak."

"Hello, I'm here. Ask me, if you want to know how I feel."

There was an astonished look from Tan Rue and a thin smile from the one he had called Master.

"We only have until tomorrow. See to it that she is ready." With this, he turned and left the room.

For a while there was silence and that only because Alma was speechless.

"Lady . . ."

"Alma," she interrupted him.

"Alma," he conceded, "would you . . ."

"See if I can find my legs," she finished for him. Alma turned in her chair and holding on to its back and the table, she slowly rose. "Well, they're working," she said and took several tenuous steps. "Now, what am I supposed to be fit for?"

"There will be a ceremony and you are expected to participate in it."

"Am I going to be the sacrificial lamb?" she asked, somewhat humorously, but inwardly feared some such intentions might be in store for her. She felt some relief in their calm and kind nature.

Tan Rue began to laugh. "Forgive me, La . . . Alma. No, you are not going to be sacrificed."

After being shown to a much needed bathroom with a toilet behind a privacy screen, Alma went through her yoga asanas, and some walking around the room. By evening, her muscles were more responsive to her demands.

CHAPTER TWO

Morning came, or was it noon? Alma had no idea. Her sense of time was totally mixed up. Had she eaten breakfast yet or not? She sat up. It was still the same bed and the same room.

Haven't been demoted yet, she joked to herself, partly to help alleviate her growing apprehension.

Still feeling sleepy, she returned to the bed and easily fell asleep. The next time she awakened was from voices in the room. Tan Rue came up to her bed, and as before, handed her a glass with the same golden liquid. "Lady, it's time to rise," he informed her.

"What are these people doing in here?" she asked in a whisper.

"It's time to get ready for the ceremony."

Alma gave Tan Rue a long look. She knew evasion when she heard it. Slightly apprehensive, she left the bed worrying . . . why was she never given a straight answer or told in what kind of ceremony she was about to participate.

Tan Rue led her to the bathroom where she appreciated the privacy screen.

"No door, but at least modern enough," she mumbled. With a shudder she remembered the outhouse at her grandmother's place. Then she nearly chuckled. Her great-grandmother was adamant she was not going to have something smelling like that in her house. To her dying day she used the outhouse. Her grandmother agreed with her own mother until she saw how it worked, then couldn't wait to have one installed.

When Alma came out from behind the screen, she was dealing with the shock at the lack of hair on her groin and legs, and when she came face to face with her reflection in a floor length mirror, her mouth dropped and both her hands flew to her head. No hair! She raised her arms and ran her hands along her arms . . . none, anywhere. When she peered closely into the mirror, not even eyebrows. Furious, she was about to turn on Tan Rue when she noted that the bags under her eyes were gone. Her skin was smooth and her face younger by years.

Alma was not tall, but above average for a woman and slender. Her hair, when she had had any, had been black and her eyes dark until she turned toward the light. They were a startling, luminous gray.

"Naturally, you won't tell me how all this happened," she said icily.

"Lady, please," Tan Rue said, somewhat discomfited. He pointed to what looked like an A-frame, and there was a floor-drain under it.

"What am I supposed to do with that?" Alma demanded, drawing on the courage from her past, dealing more assertively with her apprehension. She raised her chin as she stepped up to Tan Rue and allowed him to unbutton her nightgown. It fell to the floor.

"Please take hold of the horizontal bar."

Unabashed, she stepped over the nightgown and reached for the top bar. When Tan Rue began to wet her down with a shower wand, she couldn't help saying. "First shorn and now made ready for the sacrifice."

Tan Rue turned the water off and went down on one knee trying to quell his laughter. "Lady, you are going to get me into trouble," he was finally able to say.

The next thing he did was to soap her down. When he came to her more private areas, she let go of the bar and froze. Turning her head, "My mother taught me how to wash myself," she informed him hurriedly. She didn't get what he mumbled, but he continued with the ablution. When it came to toweling her dry, his hands were not very shy either. Alma had to keep herself from flinching and suppressed a grin.

"I'm dry; now what?"

"Please, would you come over here," Tan Rue asked, pointing to a massage table. After she had lain down, he rubbed scented oil into his hands. Alma raised her head, "Mmm, smells good," she conceded.

After rubbing down her back, he asked her to turn over.

Somewhat reluctantly, she complied. His hands moved in a very detached and professional manner across her breasts and down her abdomen.

"You're a monk, right?"

"Yes, my L . . .

"Alma."

"Yes, Alma."

"Now what?" she asked after he completed his task.

"Please follow me."

He led her back into the bedroom and there still were the three monks. Standing somewhat self-consciously in her birthday suit, she mumbled, "No blemishes?"

The old monk, whom Tan Rue had called Master, asked, "What is she talking about?"

"A sacrificial lamb."

"More or less," the old monk told her, dryly.

Taken aback, Alma looked at him. "I think it's about time you told me what's going on and where in the devil's name am I?"

"Profanity will get you nowhere," he told her sternly and turning to Tan Rue. "Now get her dressed."

Tan Rue went to get a black dress with a voluminous skirt and put it on her.

"No underwear?" she mumbled.

Tan Rue only gave the Master a long, suffering look while he had her slip on shoes. After she was dressed, he placed a heavy black veil over her head. It covered her whole body.

Alma felt her hackles rise. Looking at the silent monks and the black attire gave her a feeling of impending doom. Only self-preservation pressed her to go along with these preparations.

Hemmed in between the Master and another monk, she was led down a long corridor to a door that opened at their approach. The room was empty except for a raised platform. On it stood a high-backed chair.

"Please, take a seat," the Master told her.

Once she was seated and the folds of her dress and veil were arranged, the Master informed her that the platform would rise and for her not to be frightened by its movement.

"You will find yourself in a plaza full of people. Don't allow that to disconcert you. I will tell you when to rise and then I will give you a chalice. You will carry the chalice down a walkway to its center where you will find a woman reclining on a divan. You will give the chalice to her. After she has taken a drink, you will take three steps backward, turn, and come back to this chair."

The Master had barely finished, when the platform began to rise. Despite the warning, Alma's face revealed a moment of alarm as it rose for several seconds before coming to rest. It was past noon, the sunlight already slanting toward the horizon. The platform merged with a large plaza thronging with people. Suddenly, the murmuring abated and the crowd fell silent. Everyone turned to face the platform.

Alma had no time to reflect on the proceedings.

"Now, rise slowly," she was ordered by the Master.

Alma rose as slowly and dignified as she could. The veil was pulled away from her face and she was given the chalice.

As she walked slowly down the aisle, she could feel the tension of the crowd. She was frightened more by what she didn't understand than the number of people. What was the purpose of all this? Why and how had she been chosen in the first place? If she could have run, she would have. As she moved closer, the woman's face became clear. It was intense and focused on Alma's approach. When Alma reached the center, she realized the setup was stage-like.

The woman was indeed reclining on a divan in front of a low table on which sat an enormous flower arrangement and a few dishes of fruit and sweets. Three men were sitting in a semicircle of chairs along one side of the table. The woman turned her face up towards Alma; she appeared drained and ghostly pallid. The men were despondent.

Alma stopped mid-motion, not quite offering the chalice. She had a sudden feeling of disquiet and outrage. What kind of bizarre drama is this . . . . I have no clue . . . . no script. Is it dread . . . or panic . . . I feel?. A prod in her back reminded her to continue the motion of handing the chalice to the woman.

The woman looked into Alma's face. At first it was hatred, perhaps, then . . . is it pity? Alma wondered.

The woman took a deep swallow from the chalice and with a look of pure hate handed it to one of the men.

Alma looked away, feeling sorry for the men, not knowing why. She took the required three steps backward and with an uneasy feeling, turned to walk back to her chair.

The time passed slowly as Alma sat in the chair. She watched the people center stage. Every once in a while the woman would reach for the chalice or sweets. There was music, interspersed by a sonorous voice reading verses from a large book. As soon as the sunlight touched the horizon, all sounds ceased. It was an eerie feeling as if all the people were holding their breath. When the light finally slipped below the horizon, a choir began to sing. The voices were low, monotone, and halting . . . it reminded Alma of a requiem.

Four monks dressed in black robes with their cowls pulled over their heads came down another walkway. The Master, leading the procession, walked with measured steps toward the center.

Apprehensive, Alma observed the Master first bending over the woman and then the three men. When he raised his hand, the music swelled to a crescendo, then abruptly stopped. A deep toned gong was struck four times, reverberating around the plaza. The platform on which the four people rested began to rise high into the air. Only then did Alma notice the huge pile of wood. There was a solemn chant as one of the monks lit a torch and cast it onto the wood. It must have been impregnated with oil for it immediately caught fire and quickly burst into an inferno. Then the platform was lowered slowly down upon the pyre.

Alma's hand flew to her mouth. She finally understood. The chalice had contained a poison. She had carried death to those four people. Before she could move to express her outrage at what she had been made a party to, a hand with an iron grip pinned her in place.

Helpless, she stared into the flames.

She almost gasped when her platform slowly began to descend.

When she arrived at the room below, she came out of her chair with her hands raised and rounded on the Master.

He seized her hands in his and held them firmly, but not harshly. There was a stern look. "Be patient a little longer and all will be explained," she was told.

Rebellious, she opened her mouth to protest, but his icy stare quelled her outburst. She subsided when two monks grasped her by her arms. She was led back into the bedroom and given into the hands of Tan Rue. When the door closed behind the Master, Tan Rue told her, "You have only four hours, so use them to sleep," and he handed her a glass filled with what looked like water.

When she took the glass with some reluctance, he smiled. "It will calm you and make you drowsy enough to fall asleep."

Chapter Three

Alma didn't know what had awakened her. When she opened her eyes the room was in semi-darkness. She drew a long breath, afraid for what this awakening would bring.

"Lady?" Tan Rue's whisper came from the foot of her bed. "I have laid out a repast for you before you need to be dressed." When he turned the lights up, Alma could see a small round table laid out with a meal. As she slid off the bed, he put a robe around her shoulders.

Alma turned to him and placing her hands on both sides of his face, she made him look at her. "Tan Rue, please tell me what is going on? And what am I doing here? All this frightens me. I feel helpless. I'm caught up in something I don't understand."

"Lady, all I can tell you is that everything will be all right. There's nothing for you to worry about. Everything will be explained," he assured her. When she sat down at the table, he handed her a glass.

Taking the glass, she squinted at it. "What's in it?"

"Nutrients to balance your metabolism."

While she ate, he went to a closet and rolled out what looked like a dressmaker's dummy into the middle of the room. The dress draped on it looked stiff, made of heavy silk. It glistened with gems and elaborate gold embroidery.

As soon as she finished eating, he beckoned her to follow him into the bathroom where he gave her a toothbrush.

"I'm allowed to brush my own teeth?" she asked him.

After she brushed, he unbuttoned her nightgown and pointed to the A-frame. Again she was lathered down. After she was toweled dry, he handed her something that looked like bloomers, the legs going all the way down to her ankles; her under dress was made of soft, but thick material.

After she donned her underwear, she was led back into the bedroom and asked to sit in front of a mirror where Tan Rue applied makeup to her face. When she was finally able to inspect his handy-work, she was taken aback. The makeup was so thick, it almost obscured her features like a mask.

Before she could complain, the door opened and the Master and his monks came back in. At least this time, he waited until I was a little more dressed, Alma thought.

Two of the monks lifted the jeweled dress off the dummy and the Master motioned for them to dress her. When the dress came to rest on her shoulders, Alma nearly staggered.

"I think I would like a little less glitz and glitter," she complained to the Master.

The Master only grunted, neither irritated nor amused.

After Tan Rue put high-heeled shoes on her feet, she took some tentative steps. Not bad. The shoes were soft and fitted like they had been made for her.

The dress billowed out like the gowns her great-grandmother used to wear to a ball. As a young girl, she had dreamt about wearing such finery, and dancing in the arms of her prince charming. But for this dress, she felt no liking. It was stiff and difficult to move in.

"Whoever designed this dress should be made to wear it," she mumbled under her breath.

She was ignored and only told, "Please follow me," by the Master.

Alma was led to another room, empty except for several showcases. Under the glass-covers were jewelry, necklaces, wristbands and rings. Another contained tiaras and crowns.

Alma gasped as her hand went across the glass. "Oh, how beautiful," she whispered.

"Select what you would like to wear," the Master told her.

"You mean I can actually have one of these?"

"Yes. Anything your heart desires."

Alma picked up an emerald necklace, the stones ringed by tiny pearls. She let it run through her fingers and then gently put it back again. There was a gold necklace made into filigree with matching earrings.

"I would like to have these," she said.

"Are those all you wish to have?" the Master asked.

"The dress is glitzy enough, but these are lovely."

"Now select a crown. Which one would you prefer?"

"What would I want with a crown? I don't mind taking the necklace and earrings, because they are beautiful. And now I really would like to go home. This charade has lasted long enough."

"No charade, my Lady, and you are home. Now select a crown. Which one would you like?"

Alma looked at the crowns. Most of them were elaborate. I bet they would be heavy to wear and give you a headache to boot, she thought. She pointed to a golden circlet with an opalescent stone in its center.

"I think this one would be just about heavy enough," she told the Master.

"You may wear the earrings and the necklace," she was told.

Tan Rue fastened the earrings onto her earlobes and then gave her a hand-held mirror. "Are they to your liking, or would you want to wear something else?" he asked, as he pointed to the jewels in the showcase.

"No, these are fine," she replied, admiring the earrings in the mirror.

"What name would you choose other than your own?"

"Alma has been good enough for me. My mother gave it to me."

"Just for the sake of the game, choose another."

"Game?" Alma asked. "Is that what we have been playing, a game?" A game, she thought. She only felt uncertainty and being caught up in something she didn't understand.

"If it pleases you to call it a game. Now what name would you choose?"

Alma looked at herself in the mirror. Gray Eyes was what her father had called her. As a child, she had been as skinny as a reed and her large gray eyes were the dominant feature of her face.

"Bortei," she said and smiled as she examined her eyes.

"All right, Lady Bortei, now it is time to continue," the Master said.

They entered the room with the platform at its center and this time the chair was somewhat more elaborate. It was high-backed like the other had been but more ornate and was covered in red velvet.

She sat down and was told to compose herself. As her platform rose, there came a sudden high note from a trumpet. When the platform stopped, Alma realized it was the same plaza, but from a different angle. Suddenly, another platform rose up from the ground amid a renewed trumpet blare. Like her chair, it became part of a wide landing between marble stairs.

"Don't turn, just look straight ahead," someone whispered into her ear, and pulled down at her dress. It had been a command. I must leave! I must get away! The thoughts came with a sudden urgency. She was about to rise, but was halted by a command. She sat still and did not move. Too late, she thought, it's too late. She felt like a puppet without volition, pulled around by strings. She stared out at a sea of solemn faces looking up, not a single smile among them.

The voices of children rose in a song as an aisle formed, and young girls in white gowns came walking stately up the stairs. Then they parted and were positioned along the outsides of the two chairs. The Master, dressed in purple and gold, suddenly appeared and stood between them. He put the circlet Alma had chosen on her head.

"Behold the Lady Bortei, Queen of Atlan," his voice rang out. Then turning to the other chair, he announced, "Behold the Lord Minyar, High-Priest of Atlan."

Trumpets blared, and cymbals clashed as the crowd roared. Alma sat frozen in the chair, first in bewilderment, then in anger as she glared up at the Master.

"What's this nonsense?" she hissed. Looking at him, her eyes began to flash.

"You heard, now sit still," he had the affront to whisper back.

The rite of marriage was performed and at its end, Alma and the High-Priest were asked to rise. For the first time, she looked at him. He was taller than she and lean. Driven by curiosity, she slowly raised her eyes. His face was sensitive with deep-set, light-brown eyes. He looked as solemn as the occasion required, but there was a twinkle in his eyes. When she came to his head she had a hard time suppressing a grin; his was as bald as hers.

On Alma's dress hung two tassels. The Master took one of hers and one from the High Priest and lightly entwined them.

"Now you are joined. The State and the Temple are one in purpose. One in binding Atlan to the precepts of Heaven," the Master intoned. Then he loosened the tassels and let them fall.

Both returned to their respective thrones. Only the High-Priest sat down and Alma was told to remain standing.

Now what, she thought, beginning to tire of the game.

The Master called out a name and a man rose. He, too, was tall and slender. As he ascended the stairs, Alma could see his dark complexion and dark eyes. He stopped one step below the landing, then kneeled and bowed low before her.

"Rise, Sinuhe, Prince of Lazar.

The man rose and the Master put a heavy purple robe across his shoulders.

"Prince Sinuhe, the Oracle has named thee, Governor of Atlan.

To Alma's consternation, another rite of marriage was performed and she looked bleakly at the Master. For the first time, Alma became aware of another chair, or call it a throne, she thought, standing one-step below. Two monks pushed it so it stood below her, not quite center, but offset to her right.

After Prince Sinuhe took his seat, the nobles of the land walked by one by one, bowing in reverence.

Alma sat upright, not knowing what was holding her up. When the platform had risen to the plaza, the sunlight had just come over the skyline. Then it was mid-way up in the sky. When the procession of the nobles was over, it had nearly descended to the horizon. She was spent and weary. There was a feeling of unreality to it all. She was so tired, all she desired was sleep and for this to be a dream, for her to wake up in her own bed.

She must have dozed. Suddenly the platform descended. When it stopped in the room, Alma rose with the help of Tan Rue. She felt stiff and sore all over. She looked strained and tired.

"Come my Lady," Tan Rue said and solicitously led her out of the room and down a dimly lit corridor.

She followed him into a vestibule, and from there through double doors into a spacious room from which other rooms led away.

The Lord Minyar stood at the threshold of one of the rooms, and she noticed he had changed out of his ceremonial garb into an off-white robe.

As she approached, she looked up at him. There seemed to be a definable quality about him; he emanated power. His face reflected strength and imagination. He was tall and very attractive, dark-complected with lively, light-brown eyes that gave the impression they saw everything. His nose was straight and long, his lips, well formed.

"Lady Bortei," he said, stepping back. He had a clear, confident voice. The room was sparsely furnished and a table was laid out with refreshments. "Would you like to sit? I bet you're starved."

Alma looked at him and then at Tan Rue. "I would if I could. Tan Rue, would you help me step out of this dress?"

Scandalized, Tan Rue looked to Lord Minyar, who only chuckled.

"Tan Rue, there's a robe in one of the closets about three doors down. I think this would suffice for modesty," Minyar told him.

After Tan Rue departed, Alma turned to the Lord Minyar. "I'm sorry, but this dress weighs a ton and is so stiff, I can hardly move."

Amusement tucked at the corner of his mouth when he replied, "I can believe it."

Tan Rue returned with a robe draped over his arm. Alma told him, "Now just unbutton the back so I can step out."

After Tan Rue unbuttoned the back, Alma slipped her arms from the sleeves and stepped out of the dress and left it standing upright. She was quickly wrapped in the robe before Tan Rue moved back.

"Oh, my goodness. I feel like I'm floating," Alma exclaimed once she took the first few steps free of the dress.

"Now would you care to share these refreshments with me?" the Lord Minyar asked.

"Gladly." Alma sat down and the Lord Minyar waved Tan Rue aside and began serving her himself.

Only after swallowing her first bite, did Alma realize how famished she was. Her last meal had been very early that morning.

When her first hunger was assuaged, Alma leaned back in her chair and gave the Lord Minyar a studied look. "So," she said, "you're the High-Priest?"

"Yes. And you are the Queen," he replied, obviously amused.

"That's crazy. I'm Alma and I come from . . . where in heaven's name did I come from?"

"From heaven."

"Yeah, sure. Please, quit with this farce. It has been going on long enough."

Unnoticed by both of them, the door had opened and an elderly monk had come in. "It is no farce, Lady Bortei."

Annoyed at the interruption, Alma asked," Where is the Master? I have some questions for him. He has been orchestrating this thing long enough. Now, I would like to have some answers."

She could see the older monk's mouth quirk. "Lady Bortei, his job is done. He was only required to get you ready."

"Lady Bortei, may I introduce the Lord Manetho, your adviser," the Lord Minyar said.

"Lord Manetho." Alma inclined her head. "I think it would help us all, especially me, to start from the beginning. I'd like to know how in the world I got here and why?"

"May I sit down?" Manetho asked.

"I'm sorry. Please do. But then, it's not my place," she said as she looked at the Lord Minyar.

"It's not mine, either," he informed her.

Exasperated, Alma huffed out through her cheeks.

"Lord Manetho, I think you ought to begin," the Lord Minyar suggested.

The Lord Manetho took the next chair. "Lady Bortei, on my world, an Oracle speaks and we are directed to a world, a place, to find the next Queen. We were directed to your world and the precise place where you were and then brought you here."

Alma stared at him speechlessly. An Oracle! What's this? A lot of religious mumbo jumbo, she thought. "How does this Oracle envision me to know how to govern a land or a people?"

"It is my job to counsel and guide you. Then Prince Sinuhe has been groomed all his life to govern . . ."

Bortei took a deep breath. "Am I just to be a figure head?"

"No, Lady Bortei, you reign absolute."

She stared at Manetho and then at Minyar. "Ab . . . you mean my word is law? That's even crazier than I imagined."

"With our guidance and help . . ."

She pushed out her chair, then stopped. "I would like to speak to this Oracle. I want to know why in God's name it picked me." Now Alma was furious and too angry to be deterred as she looked from one man to the other.

"That's not possible . . ."

The door burst open and the Master strode in. "Yes, I'm told it's possible," he said, indignantly. There was no precedence. No one had ever spoken to the Oracle, who was considered sacrosanct.

Alma jumped from her chair, "Good, let's go," she said undaunted. She would see this Oracle. She had always been skeptical of psychics and fortunetellers. In ancient times people had relied on such prophets and believed in them. But, not now.

Alma hurried out of the room before anyone could stop her. She didn't know where she was or where she was going. She rushed down a barely lit corridor with the Master close behind. She went to the end of the corridor and up a long flight of stairs. There were several sharp corners to turn. Somehow, she knew where to go. After taking another flight of stairs, she came to a golden door. It opened by itself and fell shut behind her.

The room was huge and she was drawn to the only light source. It came from an ancient oil lamp which stood in an alcove. Alma hesitated, then walked slowly toward it until a weak force field stopped her. Surprised, she halted to think for a moment, then sat cross-legged on the floor.

There was a slight hesitation, then she ventured, "I have come to ask a question."

"What is your question?" a voice asked, sounding in her head.

Startled, Alma swallowed. Wow, she thought, that's interesting. Taking a deep breath, she asked, "Why me? And who are you?"

Alma heard a slight chuckle. "I'm the Oracle and you fit the job description."

Alma's mouth dropped. No obscuring language. No thee and thou. That's a new one, she thought. "Are you embodied or disembodied?"

Again, a chuckle. "I have been disembodied for many eons. I will guide you. Only go into meditation, as you know how to do. I will always call you Alma and accept the name Bortei."

Suddenly it dawned on her. "I have heard your voice before," she told the Oracle.

"Yes. I have been instructing you and was teaching you our language."

"But I don't remember anything."

"You will remember when needed."

Alma sat for a while in silence, digesting what she had learned, then rose. The door opened for her and when she stepped out, the Master was waiting for her.

He looked at her in astonishment. She was still alive and well.

"Now lead me back to the others," she told him.

***

When the door opened, the Lord Minyar was by himself. Tan Rue was either gone or invisible.

"Lady Bortei?" Rising from his chair, there was an unasked question.

"I am well," she assured him. Then looking at the big glass door, "Is there an outside?" she asked.

"Of course," he said and walking to the door, he opened it for her.

"It's already dark," she said, surprised and went out into a small walled-in garden with a mountain in the background. There was a flagged patio and a walkway leading up to a parapet.

Alma walked up to the parapet and looked down. She could barely make out the houses, but some of the windows shone with a dim, golden light. Sitting on the parapet, she wondered at this. Then, looking up at the sky, she searched for the few constellations she knew, but they were not there.

Disappointed, she sighed.

The Lord Minyar had come up silently beside her. "Lady Bortei?" he inquired.

"I thought maybe . . ."

Discerning the sigh, he asked. "You find yourself farther from home than you thought?"

"Yes. Nothing looks familiar. Not even the sky." Pointing down, "What city is this?"

"Azzan, the largest city on Atlan. Lady Bortei . . ."

"Please, drop the Lady and just call me Bortei."

"If you drop the Lord."

Alma smiled at him, "Gladly," she told him. "That makes it easier to ask intimate questions."

"What is it you would like to ask me?"

"I wondered if you have any idea of how little was explained to me. I was just told to do this or say that. All off a sudden I found myself called Queen. To top it off, I have acquired two husbands. Tell me, is this so-called marriage between religion and state, figurative or otherwise?"

"It is figurative and otherwise. The marriage has to be consummated."

"Oh, my goodness," she said, taken aback. Then her eyes were suddenly sparkling with mischief. "Do we have time to get acquainted first?"

"Three days," he said with a broad grin.

Alma glanced quickly up at him then jumped off the parapet. "Short courtship," she quipped.

Minyar laughed. "Let's go inside. I think Tan Rue is waiting for us."

"Who and what is he?"

"He is your bodyguard and servant."

"I thought he was only my shadow."

Minyar took her hand, the first time he had touched her. "That, too," he told her, raising her hand to his lips.

Tan Rue stood waiting for them just inside the door. "Would my Lady like for me to remove her makeup?" he asked.

Her hands immediately touched her face. "I forgot all about that," she said. "Yes, please."

She was led into a bathroom where a chair stood facing a large, three-sided mirror. After he was finished removing her makeup, he pointed to the now familiar A-frame. Alma gave a deep sigh, then submitted to the procedure.

Dressed in her nightgown, Alma gave Tan Rue a suspicious look. This one was a little more seductive than the ones she had been wearing lately.

"Please, this way my Lady," he told her, opening another door into a bedroom. The bed was big with the covers folded back on both sides.

Oh, she thought, that's how the wind blows. Self-conscious, she sat down on the edge with her back to the door.

"Bortei?" a soft voice asked.

Startled, she turned. It had taken a moment to register that *she* was Bortei

Minyar stood in the doorway watching her. As she looked at him, she thought, I need to begin thinking of myself as Bortei.

Minyar came in, and like her, sat down on the edge of the bed. He took her hand. "I know you are tired; if you like, I will sleep in another bed."

Bortei looked at him and then at the bed. "It's big enough for both of us."

Toward morning, she turned and realized that there was a warm body beside her. She first thought of Sep, her husband, but then immediately remembered where she was. She touched Minyar lightly, and he answered her touch by turning toward her and pulling her into his arms.

Bortei was surprised she could still respond so ardently.

CHAPTER FOUR

Minyar sat by the window while Bortei was still asleep. Tan Rue walked silently up to him, handing him a folded slip of paper.

He opened the missive and read, astonished. It was a summons to meet with the Lord Manetho. He rose carefully so as not to waken the Queen and followed the messenger who had handed the note to Tan Rue.

Manetho was waiting, but not in the temple as he had surmised, but in one of the anterooms to a smaller audience chamber. When he entered, Manetho and Master Ashir rose.

"I'm sorry to disturb you Minyar, but we have a situation developing. Your brother, Lorn, has made good on his threat. He is leading an uprising to depose the Queen," the Lord Manetho explained.

"To depose the Queen? Is he insane?" Minyar exclaimed.

"He claims that all the stories about the Oracle and the Silent Ones are a myth the priesthood promulgates to stay in power."

"Does he not know that I am High-Priest?"

"Apparently not."

"Unfortunately, I lost contact with him a long time ago. His drive and ambition got in the way of any family feelings. I often thought he was demented."

"That might be so. We need to get the Queen away from here, to a place he won't suspect."

"What have you decided to do?"

"Lord Minyar, we cannot make a move until we know where Lorn is," Master Ashir said.

"All right. I need to get back before she awakens. I'll let you know through Tan Rue what we decide to do."

"Is the marriage consummated?"

"It is, Master Ashir." There was a smile on Minyar's face which he quickly hid from Master Ashir's eyes, but the Lord Manetho had seen it and there was a quick glance exchanged. Minyar didn't mind Manetho seeing that he had been pleased with the encounter. But Master Ashir was a different matter.

The Silent Ones were an Order of association by degrees. Minyar had joined them after he left his family, interested in the knowledge and science they taught, but the level he belonged to was considered more of a laity. Manetho, however, was of a higher degree. The Silent Ones served the Oracle. Then there were the Hidden Ones, who were commonly considered a myth as no one in the memory of Atlan had ever seen them. But Minyar knew they existed and that they worked through intermediaries like Ashir. While Manetho was human, Ashir was not. Minyar surmised that in some way the Hidden Ones had mixed their genes with some of the people of Atlan to produce the mediators. He often worried about their ultimate intentions.

When he returned to the bedroom, Bortei was still asleep. Minyar sat back down in his chair by the window and waited.

***

When Bortei first woke up, she was confused about where she was. She thought of being home, but the bed was too nice, both spacious and soft. No, I'm not home, nor am I Alma anymore. I am Bortei, and this is Atlan. I'm Queen of Atlan. Yeah, Queen. She had to shake her head. Nuts, she thought.

"Bortei?" a soft voice broke into her thoughts.

Minyar, she thought. Then she thought . . . . husband. She sat up.

"Good morning," she said. "You are up early. Did you sleep well?"

"I slept well, but it is not so early."

Bortei looked at the clock. "Oh, my goodness. Is it that late?"

"Yesterday was a memorable day," he said and smiled. "I will tell Tan Rue to serve breakfast."

After breakfast, Bortei walked out into the garden toward the parapet. She was looking down into Azzan. Music and laughter drifted up to where she stood. When Minjar joined her, she expressed the desire to join in the festivities. At first, he tried to dissuade her, but recalled Manetho advising that the Queen be away from the Palace. He had a friend in town he hadn't seen for a while. He knew with all the festivities going on, his friend would be having an open house.

Watching Minyar's face, Bortei saw his frown slowly smoothing itself out. She suggested, "We could dress in simple clothes and go down there. I would like to get to know the people and see the city. I need to get a feel for what I was so abruptly dropped into."

"Yes, we might do that. We could go into Narni. Bring us clothes for that part of town," he told Tan Rue.

An undecipherable expression crossed Tan Rue's face before he quit the room. *I don't think that's what the Queen had in mind*, he thought.

***

With her face heavily made up and both dressed in fineries, their bald heads properly covered, Bortei and Minyar were conducted through long corridors and down several staircases. Bortei lost count of how many turns they had made. Finally, they passed through a massive oak door that led onto a narrow street. It seemed deserted. Houses lined both sides and she could hear only occasional voices.

A horse drawn carriage was waiting for them.

"Where I come from, a horse drawn carriage is for romantic occasions," Bortei whispered into Minyar's ear as he handed her into the conveyance.

"Consider it so," Minyar whispered back, brushing her cheek with his lips.

"Humph," Bortei snorted and plopped herself down into the seat. She looked out the small window in the door as the carriage rumbled and bumped along. The street was cobbled and in sad repair.

Bortei realized that they had come from a side street and were now entering a main thoroughfare. A large group of drunk and boisterous revelers were blocking the street. With her face flattened against the window, Bortei watched in total disbelief. Someone knocked on the carriage door and tried to open it. There were even a few indecent gestures made toward her.

"Bortei, please lean back."

Bortei looked over at him, shocked and shook her head. "Incredible," she said.

Minyar began to chuckle and pulled her away from the window.

After close to twenty minutes, the carriage stopped and Bortei leaned forward to look out. They were halted in front of a heavily fortified villa.

Recognizing Minyar, a guard waved for the gates to be opened. Their carriage rolled through the gate and about halfway up the drive, it halted. Other carriages stood parked alongside the drive.

When they entered the house, they both were amazed, Bortei more scandalized and Minyar, embarrassed. The general behaviors were not like the entertaining parties his friend used to give, but a revelry in intoxication and promiscuity. People were going in and out, standing together in the entrance hall, and several sat at the top of the stairs with a few sprawled on steps part way up. Someone recognized Minyar and moved closer to deliver a slap on the back.

"You old blackguard, where have you been?" the young man drawled, already three sheets to the wind.

"Hello, Saul. I didn't think you'd miss me."

"Well, you and Evans suddenly disappeared. It was very noticeable." It was then that Saul noticed Bortei. Well, well, well," he drawled, "you always knew how to pick 'em." Reaching for Bortei's face, he asked, "Who's this gorgeous broad?"

"She is a cousin of mine and I advise you to keep your hands off and a civil tongue," Minyar warned him.

"Aw, don't be such a spoil sport," Saul cooed and wrapped his arm around Bortei's waist. "Come with me and I'll show you a good time," he promised.

As they walked farther into the house, Minyar spotted an old friend who was also quite drunk.

"Enous, what going on here; where's Alos?"

"Oh, you don't know. He died and his last wife is celebrating her liberty. She is spending his money left and right. I'm here to see that all of it isn't wasted."

"I can see that," Minyar acknowledged.

Minyar was about to introduce Bortei, when his nephew, Rahid, pulled on his sleeve. "Zennor, please come quickly."

"Enous, you guard . . ." what name to use, "Zoe with your life."

Minyar followed Rahid into an empty room.

"Zennor, someone has recognized. I think he went to inform Lorn."

"Where is Evans?"

"You mean, the Lord Sinuhe?" he said with a grin.

"Yes. Where is he?"

"He is at the Palace."

Minyar bit down on his lip thinking about what to do. Bortei was still in the other room. He was sure unrecognized. He had to get back to her. Minyar turned to Rahid, "I'll meet you at the Palace."

***

Bortei's drunken abductor had been pulling her along into another room, and after merging into a crowd, she was promptly forgotten.

Bemused, Bortei watched the goings on. Most were inebriated and lying where they had found a space on the floor, or sprawled over couches and chairs. Many didn't behave like gentlemen. They had their hands up their not so ladylike partners' shirts or skirts, or digging down the front of their dresses. There were even a few snoring heavily.

Shaking her head, Bortei walked toward another room from where music pulsed. Couples were managing to dance while having sex.

Oh my, Bortei thought. I'm a little out of place here.

"Zoe! Zoe!" someone was suddenly yelling over the noise. Enous appeared at her side.

"Zoe?" Then he stared at her. "Not your name?"

"You think I'd come in here using my real name," Bortei temporized.

"Zennor asked me to keep an eye on you."

"Who was that military guy?"

"Oh, that was Rahid, a nephew . . . don't you know him?" he asked suspiciously.

"Enous, I'm only a poor relation. I don't hobnob with the more elite of my family."

"What are you doing here, then?"

"I wanted to find out how the other half lives."

A half-clad woman was coming toward them, weaving on unsteady legs. "Enous, if you keep ignoring me, I'm going to get pouty. And you know you don't like me when I'm pouting."

"Enous, you better take care of her. Or, you know, she'll pout," Bortei told him.

As Enous turned toward his enamored pursuer, Bortei casually slid from the room through a side door and bumped into a young servant girl.

37

"I'm so sorry, my Lady," she apologized.

She seemed wary; probably had to fend off some of the guests. Bortei looked at her and then it occurred to her; the girl was close to her height.

What's your name?"

"Dana."

"Dana, I want you to help me," she told the flustered girl. "I want you to give me one of your dresses and you can have the one I'm wearing." When the girl looked at her with a puzzled face, Bortei added, "I'm running away. They want me to marry a guy I don't like. So, are you going to help me or not?"

"I'm going to get into trouble."

"Not if you don't tell anyone. Now come, let's make the exchange."

The girl took Bortei up four flights of stairs, all the way up to the attic. The door opened into a small, dingy room where the ceiling sloped and she could only stand up in half of the room. There was an iron bedstead with a thin coverlet on top. Under the bed was a chamber pot.

The servants aren't pampered here, Bortei thought as she looked around the room. "Dana, I don't want your best dress, just an old one."

The girl looked at her. All her dresses were old. She had never had a new dress and she sure didn't have a best dress. Dana took the only other dress she had out of a tiny wardrobe and handed it to Bortei.

Once Bortei had changed, she turned to the girl and told her, "If anyone asks from where you got the dress, tell them Lord Zennor gave it to you. And to go and ask him." When she pulled her head-cover off and the girl gave a gasp, Bortei's smile was sour. She would love to still have her head of raven black hair. "Do you have something to cover my head with?"

"I have a bonnet."

"My father cut my hair off so I wouldn't run away," Bortei explained her bald head.

***

When Bortei exited the back of the house, she had no idea which direction to take. This street was also cobbled and slanted toward the middle to form a gutter. What trickled through it smelled a lot like sewer. It looked slimy and moss covered. Somewhat taken aback, Bortei stopped. While she stood in the middle of the street contemplating what to do, she was nearly run down by a horseman.

He cursed her royally.

"Girl, are you daft?" an old woman yelled.

"I hope not," Bortei told her.

"Well, if not daft, then fresh."

"Sorry, I don't mean to be. I was just startled."

"Next time walk closer to the houses."

For the first time she began scrutinizing the people. Most of the women were dressed like her, simple, ankle-length dresses made from what looked like homespun cloth. The men's trousers and tunics were made from an unbleached material. The women were carrying baskets on their arms. Some of the men had sacks slung over their shoulders.

Heeding the old woman's advice, Bortei stayed closer to the walls. She decided to follow the old woman and see where she was headed. People seemed to converge toward the same destination. Soon the street widened and Bortei found herself in a market place and began wandering around. There were primitive enclosures for pigs, live chickens and other fowl. She noticed stalls selling produce from the fields and gardens. The people were haggling lively about the prices. Someone had just butchered a pig and was selling off the parts, his customers telling him which cut they wanted.

Amused and repelled at the same time, Bortei watched the people. It definitely reminded her of a more primitive era. But how could that be? There had been electric lights, or what she had thought were electric, and modern bathroom facilities at the Temple. This place literally stank of sewer, animal offal, and rotten vegetables. She meandered paths among carts and people until, at the edge of the market, she came upon heaps of refuse. Children and women, malnourished and dirty, were digging through the garbage. The farther she walked, the dirtier the streets became and the shabbier the houses. In an alleyway, Bortei saw a whole family living in a lean-to constructed of scraps of old leather and rags. People were sitting or sleeping in doorways, others just leaned against the walls. Most of them were barefoot and covered in tattered clothes. When she continued on, she came to the edge of the market and what she saw and smelled stopped her cold. It was a sprawling slum. The odors wafting toward her were overpowering. Bortei walked on more slowly. She skirted the slum and angled back toward the city. When an oxcart passed by, she asked the old man if she could hitch a ride. Having left her fancy shoes behind with Dana, Bortei's bare feet were beginning to hurt.

She rode in the back of the wagon until he turned off toward the countryside. Again she walked for a while when another wagon, this time drawn by horses and full of young people, came abreast of her. Bortei waved at them.

"Do you want a ride?" one of the youngsters called to her.

"Yes. I have been walking so long my feet hurt."

She was hauled up into the back.

"Where are you going?" they asked.

"Into the city. I'd like to see what's going on."

"There's suppose to be dancing in the streets tonight."

"You don't say. I was also hoping I could get something to eat. They said there was free food."

"There's supposed to be a lot of that. The new Queen seems to be generous."

"That's a new one on me," Bortei replied.

There was laughter all around.

When they arrived in the city, Bortei stayed with them for a while, then got herself lost.

She was headed around the side of another hill, thinking she recognized the mountain beyond it. Suddenly she stopped. Before her, the Palace and Temple rose to an impressive height. The Palace, from the base to its top, counted twenty stories, the same as the temple. She could see now that during the ceremony she had been mid-way up, unable to discern the immensity of the structures.

People were ascending and descending the steps to the Palace doors.

Open house, Bortei thought, amused and began to climb up the stairs with the rest of the populace.

***

When Minyar went back to the party, he found Enous passed out with a female draped around his neck, and Bortei was nowhere to be found. He searched for her throughout the house, exuding vile expletives.

"Zennor, I had no idea you used words like that," one of his former friends said, slightly scandalized.

"Roe, have you seen the woman I came in with."

"No. Come to think of it, she left before Enous passed out."

"Did you see where she went?"

"She went upstairs with one of the servants."

"Are you sure she went upstairs with a servant? Do you know which one?"

"Tall, skinny, brown hair . . ."

Suddenly, an argument exploded upstairs that could be heard throughout the house. There was a slap and an outcry.

Minyar took the stairs by twos until he came to the first landing. A servant girl, wearing Bortei's dress, was crouched against the banister, shielding her head from further blows.

"I'm not lying," she sobbed. "She wanted one of my dresses and she gave me this one."

"Wait a minute," Minyar injected quickly and stayed the woman's hand. "You're Alos's widow?"

"Yes, why do you ask?"

He eyed her curiously, noticing the overly painted face and the generous décolleté that not only bared the neck and shoulders, but plunged all the way down to show her navel. "I'd like to question this girl if you don't mind."

"I do mind. This is my house."

"I know. But I think she's telling the truth." Minyar turned back to the girl. "The lady asked you to exchange dresses with her?"

"She said that she was running away from home because her father wanted her to marry a man she didn't like. She wanted to get away before she was discovered."

"A likely story," Alos's widow spouted, derisively.

A very good one, Minyar had to admit, keeping his face bland. "Could be a true story," he proposed mildly. "Do you know where she was going?" he asked the girl.

"No. She told me that if I get in trouble, to call on the Lord Zennor; he would help me."

"I am Zennor, and you can keep the dress."

"She might keep the dress, but she won't stay in this house. I don't like sly bitches around me," the widow stormed.

Minyar winced. Alos had sure made a big mistake when he married this tainted bit of goods. After the death of his first wife, he had become the marrying kind. I guess he couldn't stand being by himself. Minyar reached down to help the girl up. "Come with me. I think I can find a place for you."

They left the house in hurried strides; the girl was barely able to keep up with him. Outside the house, Tan Lar, who belonged to Tan Rue's order, was waiting for him with a horse.

"My Lord." He stopped when he saw the girl. "Our Lady has been spotted and we think she is on her way back to the Palace," he added.

"Good." Turning to the girl, he asked, "What's your name?"

"Dana, my Lord."

"Tan Lar, take Dana back with you and tell Tan Rue to find a position for her."

Minyar mounted the horse and rode off toward the Temple. When he entered the vestibule, a temple servant approached him.

"Lord Minyar, Master Ashir asked to see you. Would you please follow me?"

43

He was led to the room Master Ashir used when he was at the Temple. It was deeper than the dungeons of the Palace and not easily accessible. When the door opened, Ashir was standing by a desk with his head bowed, deep in thought.

"My Lord," Minyar said.

"Ah, there you are," he responded.

"Master Ashir."

"The Lady Bortei is at the Palace and on her way here. For the time being, you two can use my room here. Again, your brother, Lorn, has been spotted in Azzan. We will try to apprehend him."

"He's a misguided, misogynic fool. He is only doing this because he hates woman." With a bitter downturn to his mouth, he added, "The last Queen put a strain on his temperament. She was not malleable to his wishes."

"Yes, we know. He tried to poison her and when that didn't work had her addicted to drugs. He was infuriated when she didn't choose him as the governor."

"At least she showed some discernment."

"You are not in accord with your brother?"

"No, we parted ways a long time ago. His excessive need for power and control has soured our relationship."

"I was greatly surprised when the Oracle chose Evans, or what he is called now, the Lord Sinuhe, as a helpmate to the present Queen."

"Yes, it will be interest . . ."

The door opened and Tan Rue was a step behind Bortei as she entered.

"What will be interesting?" she asked, first looking at Master Ashir and then at Minyar.

Before the Master could restrain him, Minyar asked with acerbity, "Where have you been?"

Bortei pursed her mouth and then scratched her head. "You know I'm missing my hair," she told Master Ashir in an aggrieved tone of voice. And to Minyar, "I told you, I wanted to get to know the people in the street. I had very little admiration for those at that party you took me to. I went for a walk. I found the marketplace and also the slum. I consider this one hell of a mess you have here, and I want to know what you're going to do about it."

Minyar's face reddened at the tone of voice she used toward the Master and was embarrassed by the accusation.

"Bortei, you can't just walk away without telling anyone," Minyar said, lamely.

She ignored Minyar and looked at Master Ashir. "Now, I would like to know what's going on. There's a lot of activity in the streets. Are we having a riot?"

Ashir was surprised by the astuteness in which she had judged the situation.

"Yes, we have an uprising. Not everyone is pleased with having another Queen," Ashir told her bluntly.

"Oh, I see. The last one wasn't a good ruler and someone thinks he or she could do a better job?"

"Yes, that's about it in a nutshell."

"So, what is the great plan?"

Manetho, entering the room, had heard Bortei's last remark. "There's a play. It's a new one and I think I heard the Lord Minyar mentioning that he would like to see it."

There was another probing look as Bortei looked from Manetho to Ashir and then to Minyar. "Are we stashing the Queen in an unusual place?" she quipped.

Manetho chuckled. "I think we should have listened to Tan Rue," he said. "Tan Rue is becoming acquainted with her Ladyship's unique approach in dealing with events."

"Yes, we would like to do that until we apprehend the leader . . ."

"And that is who?"

"His name is Lorn Pelias, and he is Lord Minyar's eldest brother."

Bortei stared in astonishment at Ashir. "Uhh, that's a kettle of worms!" Turning to Minyar, "Not a very comfortable position for you," she said.

"No."

"And he is against you, too?"

"He doesn't know that I am High-Priest of Atlan."

"Lord Manetho, since you are my adviser, what do you recommend we do?"

"Lady Bortei, my advice is to go to this play . . ."

"Dressed up or dressed down?" Bortei interrupted. "I'm still wearing a servant's dress," she reminded them. "Oh God!" Bortei exclaimed, "Dana! Someone has to go back to that house and make sure the girl is all right. I don't want her to get into trouble for helping me."

"She is fine, my Lady. I inherited her," Tan Rue said, aggrieved.

"Oh, so she did get in trouble, and she is here?"

"Yes, Lady Bortei."

"Well, I bet you can find something for her to do," she told Tan Rue. "Well, Lord Manetho?"

"I think dressing down would be in order. We don't want to arouse attention," Minyar answered instead.

***

The auditorium was full. Bortei, sitting close to the front, was craning her neck to see who was sitting up in the balconies. They were also full and what Bortei called the glitz and glitter was well represented. It was a full house.

"Will you sit still," Minyar admonished her. "You are calling attention to yourself."

To Minyar's shock, she drawled, "But Zennor, darling, I'm from the provinces. I'm supposed to be impressed."

He looked at her and began to grin.

She grinned back. "That's right, you're supposed to look supercilious. Attitude is what counts," she whispered just before the curtain rose.

Bortei was so engrossed in the play that when the curtain fell to signal half-time, she was blinking like an owl.

"What are we going to do now?"

"We go out to the lobby and watch what everyone else is wearing. Maybe we'll have a drink or two."

"But darling, we don't have any money. We're from the provinces. At least, I am and you're supposed to be poor. Are there people there who will know you?"

"No. Not in this part of the lobby. They are upstairs."

Bortei let out a drawn out "Oooh."

Toward the end of the play, there was a sudden rustling, then voices from the balconies rose in contention and the performance came to an abrupt halt.

"What is it?" Bortei asked.

"I don't know, yet."

"The entrances are blocked by soldiers. They won't let anyone leave," someone told him.

In agitated murmurs, the news passed swiftly along the rows.

The balconies cleared one after another. Almost an hour later the people in the auditorium began to move.

Bortei pulled Minyar's head down and whispered in his ear, "We need to play the part. You're my cousin who promised to show me the town. I'm Zoe from the provinces, a poor relation of yours. I've never been in Azzan. And you better think of a last name for yourself and me."

"All right, you're Zoe Alton from Sardas, an island off the southern end. I will keep the name Zennor, and like yours, my last name is Alton. I hope we can bring it off."

Bortei waved her hand negligently, "No sweat," she told Minyar. "I only have to play dumb and you keep up that supercilious face."

"Thanks a lot."

When they came to one of the exits, two soldiers stood guard, one on each side.

"Sir, have you any identification?" Minyar was asked.

Looking at his sleeves, "Sergeant, do you think I came to the theater with my passport," Minyar drawled.

"And the lady?"

Bortei looked at the Sergeant with bright and curious eyes.

"Do you always have so much excitement? What happened? Did a murderer get loose?" she asked breathlessly.

"Where is she from?" he asked Minyar.

"Sarda. She's never been in Azzan," Minyar said, grinning.

"Oh. A country bumpkin."

"I'm afraid so."

"How come she is with you?"

"A poor relative. I thought to give her the tour. The coronation and all that, you know."

"Since you have nothing to identify yourself, I will have to detain you."

"That's going to be a long wait. You see, I'm from Coroban and that's a long ways off."

"I still have to detain you."

"Orders and all that," Minyar said, resignedly.

"Oh, don't worry. This is fascinating. I never had so much excitement in my whole life. We're going to be detained until they find the murderer and then they will have to apologize and let us go. Just think of that," Bortei said blissfully.

"She's a bit of a romantic," Minyar explained her to the Sergeant as they were led off.

In a room set aside as a detention area, Bortei sat down on a chair with her hands folded in her lap, eager to see the next installment of this drama.

After half an hour or so, an officer came into the room.

"What are you doing here, Zennor?" he asked surprised.

"Hello, Balam. Waiting to be identified," Minyar told him.

"No papers?"

"Of course not. I was going to the theater, not overseas."

"Tell them you're going on a spy mission . . ."

"Zoe, will you please shut up," Minyar admonished, feigning disgust. "Don't listen to her; she's a nut case.

"Girlfriend?"

"Oh, no. One of my cousins."

Balam turned to the Sergeant. "I'll vouch for them. I know Zennor personally."

"Thanks, Balam, I owe you one."

When they finally arrived at Minyar's assigned apartment in the Temple, Tan Rue, as always, was waiting for her.

"How do you manage to be always waiting up for me; don't you ever sleep?" Bortei grumbled.

"Would my Lady like to have something to eat?"

"Yes, we both are famished," Bortei told him.

After they had eaten, Bortei began to feel the exhaustion from the day's activity and looked forward to her bed and sleep. It was dawn when she first woke up, and hearing Minyar breathing peacefully beside her, she fell back to sleep.

The next time it was roving hands under her nightgown, going caressingly up her body. She turned and eagerly fastened her lips to his mouth.

She had a flashing memory of her other life, her cold rebuffs of the inept fumbling and constant demand for her body. She was heartened by her rekindled passion.

CHAPTER FIVE

The next morning, Bortei's hand wandered to the space next to her and found it vacant.

"Minyar," she whispered, but it was Tan Rue who answered her.

"Lady Bortei, the Lord Minyar has assumed his duties today. He asked me to convey his good wishes and for you to have an interesting day."

"And why does his wish awaken a touch of disquiet in me," she asked Tan Rue.

"Lady, would you like to breakfast now?"

"May as well. Do I have an agenda?"

"Yes. The Lord Manetho will attend to you at your convenience."

With a mischievous gleam in her eyes and her mouth twitching, she asked, "And when will this convenience occur?"

"As soon as my Lady is finished with her morning toilette."

"Then we better proceed with the necessary program."

Before Bortei went through the now customary bathing and dressing, she asked Tan Rue to convey to the Lord Manetho her wish that he join her for breakfast.

"The Lord Manetho, anticipating your desire, has already asked me to tell you he would be delighted to join you."

"Aren't we highbrow this morning," Bortei quipped.

She was just seated when the door opened and the Lord Manetho walked in.

"Good morning, Lady Bortei."

"Good morning, Lord Manetho. Would you please join me?"

Bortei waited until he was served and both were eating before she began to ask questions.

Manetho had eyed the tablet beside her cup and inwardly smiled. She was ready to get down to business.

"What does it mean . . . the Lord Minyar has assumed his duties?" was her first question.

"He is High-Priest of Atlan and . . ."

"I understand that. But, what I would like to have clarified is our relationship and how we are to interact."

"The Temple and the Palace are different spheres. I understand that the relationship would be foremost on your mind. By assuming the duty of High-Priest, the Lord Minyar will meet you for ceremonial duties, while in private capacities, only on designated days."

With a frown, Bortei asked, "And how spaced are those designated days?"

"At long intervals. Now, on today's agenda is for you to become familiar with the Queen's apartment and the ceremonial rooms."

"Why long intervals?" Bortei interjected.

"Because of his duties."

"You're not very helpful, Counselor."

"Lady Bortei, you are the Queen. Now is the time for you, also, to assume your duties."

"Ouch," Bortei said, looking at Manetho. "I stand corrected."

"Now that we are finished with breaking our fast, we will commence with the tour."

Before they left the room, Tan Rue handed Bortei a hooded cloak. "Is that necessary?" Bortei asked Manetho.

"It could come in handy," was his dry remark.

Her interest piqued, Bortei followed him.

In their descent, the stairs were interspersed with many landings. Seeming to take them forever, they traversed along cold and damp corridors. Now Bortei understood the need for a cloak. Also, she looked suspiciously at the torches mounted along the walls. Maybe electricity hasn't reached this far down, she thought. The torches were the only apparent source of light. She coughed several times from the acrid smoke they emitted.

Finally, they came to steps leading upwards for nearly as long as it had taken to descend. They came upon a small door, which opened onto a long hallway with guards posted at intervals along the way.

"Where are we?" Bortei eventually asked Manetho.

"This is the Palace. We came through an underground passage which connects it to the Temple."

The corridor ended at large double doors. Two sentries standing guard stepped forward and opened the doors for them. Bortei sailed majestically through the anteroom into the living room only to stop short, her mouth falling open. She whirled on her axis and came face to face with Manetho. "Unbelievable. Someone lives here?" she asked, incredulous.

The ceiling of the room was elaborately ornamented. The paintings on the wall depicted young people in playful and intimate scenes and between each painting were large, gilded mirrors.

"Would you like to see the bedroom?"

Shrugging her shoulder, "I suppose."

When she entered the next room, she was unable to hold back a gasp. The bed stood high on a dais in royal splendor, framed in purple swathes of drapes beneath its canopy. The bed cover was damask and the furniture was dark and solidly heavy. There was a statue of two people in ardent embrace in one corner of the room. The paintings on the walls . . . Bortei blushed and then had to swallow hard as she examined them. Pornographic was the mildest descriptor that came to mind. Depicted were nudes, male and female, in an array of intimate poses.

She gestured to Lord Manetho. "I would never stop blushing if I had to sleep in here. I'm not a prude, but where I come from, this is in very bad taste," Bortei informed him. Her face had blushed to a crimson red.

She went to inspect the bathroom and took a step back. The bathtub had four legs that supported the tub at least half a foot above the floor. When she looked behind the privacy screen she gave a gasp, nearly knocking the screen over. At least you can sit down was her most charitable thought. It was no flush affair and she eyed the bucket behind it. It was like something she remembered her Granny had inherited. Then it dawned on her that she had seen no windows in the whole apartment.

Walking back into the living room, she spoke insistently. "Lord Manetho, it is not possible for me to live here. You will have to . . ."

She was interrupted by loud voices coming from the hallway, raised in contention. Suddenly the door burst open. A man still bellowing in a strident voice was in the forefront. His eyes roved from Manetho to Bortei.

"What have we here? The want-to-be Queen?" he shouted when he caught sight of Bortei.

"Lorn Pelias, you will conduct yourself with decorum in the presence of the Queen." Manetho's voice was calm, but authoritative.

"Manetho, when I rule Atlan there will be no place for you and your ilk!" Lorn shouted.

At the sound of voices in the hallway, Lorn abruptly lunged at Bortei, brandishing a thick-bladed knife.

The blur of a figure burst through the door and launched itself at Lorn, slamming him against a dresser, snatching at the knife. Angered by the interference, Lorn bellowed and threw the knife at Bortei. She pivoted back and caught the knife midair and adeptly returned it. The knife pierced the upper part of Lorn's shoulder, pinning him to the dresser.

Shock filled Lorn's face as he gaped at the knife, then glared back at Bortei.

"Many hours spent practicing knife throwing with my brothers," Bortei explained, almost apologetically.

There was a prolonged silence as all eyes went to Bortei.

"Lady?" Manetho asked.

"I'm all right, Lord Manetho," Bortei told him and held up both hands. Now, Bortei took notice of who else had come rushing into the room. "Lord Minyar, Prince Sinuhe," she said and inclined her head.

Both men were breathing hard and Minyar was wiping the sweat from his brow.

"I sincerely apologize for not being able to prevent my father from attacking the Queen," Sinuhe said to Manetho. "Zennor and I found out too late that he had invaded the

Palace. Rahid and his troops are rounding up my father's men. "Your Majesty, my abject apologies."

Bortei inclined her head. "Accepted."

"We will acquiesce to any punishment you mete out," Sinuhe added.

"You lily-livered pup; why don't you stand up to this whore? And don't give me any of that crap about an oracle. That's all poppycock and you know it."

Bortei had just taken a first step toward Lorn when a voice in her head said, "Alma, a tower sits on his land, constructed as a prison. Confine him there. Now, mind-call the Silent Ones; this you know how to do."

She visualized two cowled monks responding to her, and then she slowly approached Lorn.

Lorn's face went ashen when the two monks soundlessly materialized beside Bortei. Everyone else gawked at the two hooded men, dumbfounded.

"Lorn Pelias," reviled Bortei, "You will be confined to the tower on your property." Turning to Manetho, she added. "He will receive treatment so that a healing may be affected."

"You pathetic whore . . . you . . . I don't need anything from you . . . You," he shouted, spittle spewing from his mouth.

She snapped back at him, "And if you don't behave, you will scrape out kitchen pots for the rest of your life." Bortei nodded her head and the monks, with Lorn between them, disappeared.

Bortei, pale and still shaking inside, groped toward a chair and sat down. Running her hands over her face, she apologized. "I'm sorry. That was appalling."

Minyar went to her and kneeling down, took her hands from her face and held them. "Are you all right?"

"I'm shaking."

"I'm sorry. My brother has always hated women. He has been in a rage since the last Queen's decision left him humiliated. He swore to take the Throne. Her laughter sent him back to his home to mull over his options."

Looking at Manetho, Bortei said, "His anger is more than vindictiveness. Can his mind be swayed . . . mended."

"We will try, Lady Bortei."

"Thank you. Now if we can return to a bit of normalcy, if that even exists. This apartment. This is a . . . Minyar, would you take a look into this bedroom? Unless you already know what's in there."

"No, Bortei. I never had the honor of gracing her late Majesty's bedroom," he assured her as he stepped toward the door. He stopped at the threshold. "Evans, come here and look," he called to his nephew in a voice of someone greatly impressed and then chortled.

Evans walked up next to his uncle and gasped.

Coming up beside Minyar, Bortei suggested, "Lascivious."

Minyar grinned and looked at Prince Sinuhe. "Evans, what would you call it, instructive?"

Bortei studied one of the paintings then took a step away from Minyar and gave him a once over. "Umm," she said, overly contemplating him.

Minyar had the decency to blush under her gaze and Sinuhe spluttered.

"You see," she told the two, "if I slept here, I would never get over blushing."

***

Yesterday's tour, other than the Queen's apartment, included the throne room and lesser audience chambers. Manetho explained some of the ceremonies and what deportment was expected of her. He also instructed her in many of the court procedures, its etiquette, and her and Prince Sinuhe's spheres. There was so much to remember. It was late when Bortei finally returned to the Queen's apartment. Tan Rue had lit only a few candles so she wouldn't be embarrassed by the artwork. She was promised that she would only have to sleep there for one or two nights.

Bortei had also been introduced to Prince Jovan, who was a younger cousin of Prince Sinuhe and her Minister of Foreign affairs. Like all the Pelias, he was dark-complected with brown eyes. He was of medium height and had an athletic build. His movements were quick if sometimes impatient.

Prince Ariel, another cousin to Prince Sinuhe, was the Minister of Defense. His features were strong; there was intelligence and restraint in his bearing. During their interview, Bortei noticed a momentary flash of humor.

***

Bortei was not sure what woke her the next morning. She remained still and listened. There was a rustling sound in the room. When she opened her eyes, a woman's brown eyes met her gaze.

"Good morning, your Majesty," the woman twittered, her voice at least one octave too high.

Confused, Bortei stared up at her and then noticed four more women in her bedroom. As she raised her head, one woman quickly fluffed up a pillow and put it behind her back. As Bortei moved to get out of the bed, another folded the cover back. Before her feet could touch the floor, a third put shoes on them. While Bortei sat behind the privacy screen, she was startled by proffered toilet paper. Coming out from behind the screen, she found her bath water already drawn and one of the women putting in scented salts. Her towels were laid out and her dress was precisely hung ready for her to wear. She slid into the splendidly hot water and closed her eyes, enjoying the floral scent. However, when one of the women stepped up and bent down to wash her, it was too much.

"Tan Rue, you better come in here."

"Yes, Lady Bortei?"

"I will suffer only so much indignity. Now I'm asking . . . politely . . . for these ladies to leave."

"Yes, Lady Bortei. Ladies, her Majesty desires privacy in her bath," he told the bewildered women and herded them out of the room.

When the bathroom was vacated, Bortei said, "Now, Tan Rue, we are going to have an agreement. You will oversee this bathroom ceremony. I don't like women in here or around me. I will tolerate *you*. Is that clear? And who, in whatever name, are they?"

"Your Majesty, they are your Ladies in Waiting."

"Well have them wait somewhere else, please."

It is required for your Majesty to be accompanied by her Ladies."

"But not in the bathroom."

"I will convey your wishes."

When Bortei was dressed and ready, Tan Rue led her to a small dining room where breakfast was laid out on the table. As soon as she was seated, one of the Ladies poured tea and asked how many lumps of sugar she would like.

Then her tea was stirred and brought to her lips. She sipped and then a different Lady spoon-fed her a forkful of eggs. Obediently, Bortei opened her mouth. After she swallowed the eggs, another one of the women tried to feed her a bite-size piece of frosted cake.

The smell or maybe just the nervousness of the woman alerted Bortei. She grabbed her wrist and took the piece of cake from her fingers and held it up to her nose. It smelled of almonds.

Bortei was just about to speak when the door flew open and Master Ashir entered followed by a monk from Tan Rue's order, carrying a small boy, about two years old.

The Monk brought the boy to the table and handed him to his mother. With an outcry and a sob, she pulled the child into her arms.

Bortei looked at the Monk.

"Your Majesty, Lorn Pelias had the child abducted to have the mother comply with his command, which was to poison you."

Bortei looked up at Master Ashir who held out his hand for the small piece of cake. When she handed it to him, like her, he smelled it, then deftly placed it on a small plate.

"What is it?" Bortei asked.

"It is poisonous to everyone here except you. As you know, your metabolism is different. It would only have affected you like an aphrodisiac."

"Thanks a lot. Something I don't need," Bortei mumbled as she leaned back in her chair. "Master Ashir, I have a small problem I think you will be able to help me with," she said with a tiny smile. "Master Ashir, I don't want to offend my ladies, so perhaps coming from you, they will be more appeased about my need for solitude?"

Master Ashir gave her a piercing look. "If it is your wish, it will be so arranged," he said curtly.

Bortei bowed low and said, "Thank you, Master Ashir, and now about the child."

While Bortei had been speaking with Master Ashir, she had noticed how lethargic the boy was lying in his mother's arms. She bent over the mother and gently took the child. He opened his eyes, but they immediately rolled back. Touching his skin, she found it to be both hot and dry. Turning to Tan Rue, who stood nearby as always, she said, "Mix a glass of water with syrup and salt, but only as much salt as would fill the tip of a small spoon. Then puree this fruit and stir its juice into the water."

When everything was done, Bortei, took a spoon, and while supporting the boy's head, allowed a few drops of the mixture to drip into his mouth. At first he wouldn't swallow, the liquid seeping from the corner of his mouth. With the next spoonful, he began to swallow and Bortei slowly fed all of the liquid to him. She was about to give the child some of her eggs when she looked sharply at his mother. "Is the rest of the food untainted?"

His mother's shaky hand reached for her son's small, pudgy fist and her voice quavered as she said, "Yes, your Majesty, only the petit-four."

Bortei gave him some of the eggs and then let him have a sip of her water. "Later today, you can give him what he normally eats," and she placed the boy back in his mother's lap.

For some reason Bortei glanced toward the door. Lord Manetho stood there, his hands folded inside the sleeves of his habit. His head was bowed. She looked at him and then back at Master Ashir.

Bortei slowly rose from her chair and made a deep obeisance to Master Ashir. Some time ago she had sensed his great power and even though not frightened of him, she knew he merited respect, and caution.

He turned without a word and left the room.

When Bortei looked up, Lord Manetho was closing the door behind the last of her Ladies and moved toward her table.

"Bortei!" he said sharply.

She looked at him with her eyes open wide and a tiny smile emerging. "Sorry. A foot in the mouth mishap, I admit."

Manetho lowered himself slowly into a chair and shook his head. Turned toward the wall near the door, Tan Rue suddenly developed a coughing fit.

"May I invite you to breakfast with me, my Lord?" Taking a cup, she filled it with tea.

"Someday, my Lady, you will go too far," he told her, but with a softening voice.

She turned her gaze upon Lord Manetho, eyeing him intently. "There is something you may not understand, my Lord," Bortei said severely. "I am Queen. The Oracle has chosen me. The most anyone can do to me is to kill me, and I have never been afraid of death." She inclined her head and gave him a gentle smile, then handed him the cup.

***

Bortei surmised she would have to solve the dilemma with her Ladies in Waiting herself. She had noticed one of them seemed to twitter less and behave with a more practical comportment. When she asked Tan Rue, he told her that she was Lady Dorcas and was a widow. The small stipend she received in her Majesty's service supplemented her income.

"Tell her this afternoon she is invited to take tea with me."

When Lady Dorcas arrived, she bowed low and held her eyes down. "Your Majesty."

"Lady Dorcas, rise and please dispense with this courtly deportment. Etiquette is fine, but right now I would simply like to have a chat with you. Foremost, I need information to make decisions. So sit down and Tan Rue will serve us tea."

Lady Dorcas thanked her and sat carefully and stiff-backed on her chair, arranging her skirt.

Bortei waited until they both had sipped their tea before addressing her guest.

"Lady Dorcas, it is not my intention to dispense with all the services of my Ladies in Waiting. It is only that I have a need for privacy and their constant attention is not conducive to my work. It is essential for me to be acquainted with their circumstances and functions."

"Your Maj . . ."

"Lady Bortei will do."

"Lady Bortei, their function is to accompany you at all times and see to it that you are properly attired and appear at the obligatory functions."

"I see." Again Bortei smiled. "Yet, I hope it is not an essential function to assist in the intimate routine of the bathroom."

"The last Queen required it."

"You don't say," Bortei said, astonished and wrinkled her forehead.

"She demanded our constant attention."

Glancing at Tan Rue, she smiled. "I think I'm already well cared for. Now, what I have in mind is for you to act as my intermediary. You will keep me informed of events and important issues of which I need to be aware. You will, of course, organize social functions for which you will need a hostess other than yourself. Do you know of someone who could play that part?"

There was a short pause. "Yes, Lady Bortei. It is the wife of the Minister of Interior. She has pleasant social graces. She is amiable and well liked. Also, she has the money to be fashionable, and the ambition to further her position."

"Very well presented, Lady Dorcas. Are most of the Ladies financially able to meet their obligations?"

"All, except Lady Marnie. Her husband recently died and left her in very reduced circumstances. The stipend we receive does not cover her expenses. To make ends meet, she was forced to sell her husband's estate and move into a townhouse. She had to dismiss most of her servants, except the butler and his wife who have been with her since she was first married."

"I see." There was a pensive smile and the bitter memory of her own reduced circumstances in her other life. "So, if Lady Marnie were released of her duties, it would lessen the pressures put on her?"

"Yes, considerably."

"Consider it done. Is there anything else I can do?"

"There could be gifts," Dorcas suggested.

"I see. Fine. See to it. Now, how about the gossip that's going around?" Dorcas gave her a curious look. "Gossip often contains very important information and gives me an insight into how this society functions. I don't want to know all the petty occurrences."

"I understand."

For the next half hour, Bortei found out more than she had bargained for.

CHAPTER SIX

Master Ashir and Manetho were called to meet with a member of the Hidden Ones. When they entered a cathedral-like room, they saw that he was already waiting for them. He was tall, perfectly proportioned, his countenance beautiful.

Ashir and Manetho made obeisance and then waited while remaining respectfully bowed until spoken to.

When he spoke, his voice had a rich and melodious tone. "What of the new Queen?" he asked.

"She remains an unknown element while she is settling in. She has no liking for the previous Queen's decor and asked to have an apartment readied with the modern conveniences she is accustomed to. She has also asked for her Ladies in Waiting to be removed, citing the need for privacy," Ashir informed him.

"She asked to see the Oracle."

"Yes. But what transpired was witnessed by no one."

"It is unusual and has no precedence."

"Yes, my Lord," Ashir said.

"Soon I will need a psychological profile on her. You are dismissed."

Ashir and Manetho bowed themselves out of the room. Outside, only a pregnant glance was exchanged and they went their separate ways.

CHAPTER SEVEN

Bortei, still living in the previous Queen's apartment, walked back and forth with agitated strides. The windowless rooms made her claustrophobic. She was dressed in royal regalia, ready to meet with Prince Sinuhe. When he was announced, she stood in the middle of the room facing the door.

"Your Majesty," he said with a short bow and entered the room.

Bortei studied him with candid eyes. She was so tired of the endless ceremonies and today was another such occasion that required her attendance. But first she was to confer with Sinuhe, her Governor.

"Today's ceremony," he explained, "is the pledging of fealty. You need not do more than incline your head. Since I know most of them, I will handle the addressing." His arrogant assumption instantly infuriated her. She studied him with narrowed eyes. Alluding to his father, she asked sarcastically, "Prince Sinuhe, do you also aspire to become ruler of Atlan?"

Stung not so much by the words but by the manner they were delivered and what they conveyed, he felt his temper rise. Facing her, he exploded, "I'm more qualified than you ever will be to rule Atlan."

Her gray eyes were fixed on his with a stark aloofness for several moments. "I want a writ of your qualifications on my desk by tomorrow. Also, my dear Prince Sinuhe, there is a distinction between the words govern and rule. You govern; I rule."

There was a cold glare from his dark eyes, but a gentle cough from the door ended their altercation.

Manetho bowed, then came in. "Your Majesty, Prince Sinuhe, it is time to proceed to the audience hall," he reminded them with an intense look at Bortei's somber face.

There was an almost imperceptible bow as Sinuhe forced his voice to sound even. "Then let's not dally."

Bortei followed Manetho with Sinuhe two steps behind. Before entering the audience hall, a trumpet blared and Bortei rolled her eyes to the ceiling. The Hall was packed. The Nobles and their families, dressed in their fineries, rose as one when they entered.

"The Lady Bortei, Queen of Atlan," the Chamberlain announced.

Bortei slowly crossed the space to the raised throne. Sinuhe took his station next to a high-backed chair, a step below and to the Queen's right.

She stood for a moment and received obeisance from the hall.

"The Lady Bortei will receive your fealty," Manetho announced.

The first Noble to approach was the Steward of Lazar, the principality of Sinuhe's father.

He prostrated himself before the throne. "I ask the Lady's mercy," he said.

Bortei expected Sinuhe to respond, but when no response was forthcoming, she surreptitiously kicked his chair with her foot.

Sinuhe rose and after descending the two steps, lifted the Steward from the floor.

"My friend, it was expected for you to follow Lord Pelias' orders. There is no penalty attached to loyalty."

"However misplaced," Bortei finished his sentence.

It took four hours for everyone to pledge their unwavering allegiance to the Queen of Atlan.

Bortei was relieved when it was finally over. She and Sinuhe rose and left to go their separate ways. Manetho accompanied her to the previous Queen's apartment. When she let out a shuddering sigh, Manetho said, "It won't be long, Lady Bortei."

"It's not just the art work, but this whole room that feels so . . ." searching for an appropriate word, "disharmonious," she finished and shrugged.

Manetho was about to leave when the door opened and Tan Rue came in followed by Dana who had several outfits draped across her arm. When Dana recognized Bortei, she blanched, then dropped to the floor with the dresses flying.

"Dana, what in tarnation are you doing on the floor," Bortei chided her. "Now get yourself and my clothes off the floor and please don't do that again."

"Yes, your Majesty. No, your Majesty . . ."

"Stop blubbering and get up, girl. Tan Rue, did you find a place for her?"

"Yes, Lady Bortei. She will do some of the work around your apartment when it has been completed."

"Is it nearly done?"

"Yes, my Lady, soon."

"Now, let's get me out of these crazy clothes and see if what you brought fits," she told Dana.

Bortei walked into the bedroom with Dana behind her. With a loud gasp and her hand clasped to her mouth, Dana gaped at the art work.

"Exactly," Bortei said. "Now, help me out of this rigid stuff."

Once she was dressed in trousers and a loosely fitting overdress, Bortei uttered a sigh of absolute relief. Entering the other room, she asked Manetho, "Don't you think this looks a lot better?"

"Probably much more comfortable," Manetho agreed. "But you will still have to wear your ceremonial garb."

"But in my private sphere, I will wear less glitzy clothes, agreed?"

"Agreed."

"Now, where did Prince Sinuhe go off in such a hurry?"

"There is a ball later that he is required to attend," Manetho explained.

"But not the Queen?"

"No, your Majesty."

"Hmmm," she responded with a speculative look. "Dana, do you still have the dress I gave you?"

"Yes, my Lady."

"I would like to borrow it back until I have a more complete wardrobe."

"What are you contemplating?" Manetho asked, alarmed.

"Attending this ball, of course. Get me Lady Dorcas while I change my dress," she told Dana. "Come, Tan Rue, I need you to apply my makeup and I hope you have a wig for me."

She quelled Manetho's retort with a long, meaningful look.

When Lady Dorcas arrived, Bortei was dressed and Tan Rue had supplied a wig made from her previous hair.

"Lady Dorcas, do you have any poor relations who couldn't possibly make it to court."

Lady Dorcas looked at her without comprehension.

"Don't you have a poor cousin or poor niece coming to visit you?"

When Lady Dorcas continued the empty look, Bortei explained, "I'm your poor relation. You are being kind and introducing me at court, or whatever you call it. I'm dressed as you see, so I can go to this party, unrecognized. Do you understand?"

"Yes, Lady Bortei. You're my cousin Rena from Sarda. Poor people no one here would know."

"I knew you were bright; that's why I called on you. Let's go to the party. Don't say too much about me. We don't want to raise unwelcome curiosity."

When Bortei and Dorcas arrived at the ballroom, Dorcas said, "Stay close and follow me." She looked surprised when Bortei wriggled her hand into hers.

"I'm your poor relation, remember. And relax," she whispered, giving Dorcas's hand a gentle squeeze.

The ballroom was full, but not crowded. Most of the people were still in the salon standing in groups, chatting.

"The majority are not finished exchanging gossip," Lady Dorcas explained.

"That's what I'm interested in, gossip," Bortei told her.

"I see." Dorcas put a wealth of understanding in those two words. "Then we need to pass close to those three gentlemen." Dorcas steered Bortei close enough for two of the men to notice.

"Oh, Lady Dorcas," one of them hailed. "What is this about the Queen dismissing her Ladies in Waiting?"

There was a brief, "Oh," from Dorcas. "I don't know how that rumor started," she said, rather primly. "Of course, she did not dismiss her Ladies. She only informed us that she needed more privacy."

"But what reasons does she have for privacy?"

"Of course, being a man, you would not understand, Lord Garston," Dorcas enlighten him.

"Ah, the mystery of a woman's world."

"Lord Stan," Lady Dorcas reprimanded him firmly.

"Who is your charming companion?" Lord Usten asked.

"This is my cousin, Rena. She's come to stay with me for a while."

Suddenly, there was a commotion near the front of the room. Prince Sinuhe and his cousin, Prince Jovan, the Minister of Foreign Affairs, had just entered with a small entourage.

"You really think he has fallen out of favor with the Queen?" Lord Stan whispered to Lord Usten.

There was a strained smile as Lord Usten said, "You must not believe all you hear. But there's a rumor that the new Queen is going to change a few things."

"Really? I hope it is true that the arrogant, you know who, is in trouble," said Lord Stan, meaning Prince Sinuhe.

"You haven't forgiven him?"

There was a short and explosive, "No!" as Lord Stan's eyes followed Sinuhe.

"I think what you forget is that it was his father who was behind all that."

"Yes, I know. He marched as stealthy as a thief into the Rimal Mountains. You know, it's an ore-rich area my family has owned for ages and he tried to claim it for Lazar."

"He's coming our way," Lord Garsten warned them.

"He would have the gall," Lord Stan whispered, put out.

Bortei looked up. Jovan was richly, almost gaudily dressed, while Sinuhe wore a more somber garb. She quickly turned away, not wanting to be recognized. She had Dorcas introduce her to a group of ladies.

"Hello Stan," Bortei heard Prince Jovan's voice at her back. "We are glad you could come. We hope you will enjoy yourself." Then Jovan and Sinuhe greeted the other gentlemen.

"Let's go somewhere else," Bortei whispered to Dorcas.

Dorcas pointed to an open door and said, "I think we are to go into the banquet."

"Oops, I didn't think about that. How are we seated?"

"By name."

"Do I have a seat?"

"Yes, my La . . . Rena. I have placed you between two elderly bachelors."

"Thanks a lot, Dorcas. They will probably talk incessantly about the glory days of their youth."

Dorcas laughed. "Probably and right past you as if you weren't there."

"You are close by?"

"Yes, across from you."

"And the Lords?"

"Way up at the other end of the table."

After everyone had found their seat, they were still standing, waiting for Prince Sinuhe and Prince Jovan. When they finally entered the banquet hall, silence fell.

Once the two Lords were seated, there was a scraping of chairs and the clatter of dishes and silverware commenced.

As Dorcas had foreseen, the two gentlemen gave Bortei a cursory look and short bow. Then they became preoccupied with themselves, leaving Bortei free to observe the other guests.

Beside the two princes sat two lovely young ladies with whom the two were having lively conversation. Prince Jovan quite often broke out in loud laughter and would intimately lean toward Prince Sinuhe's table partner. Suddenly Bortei's attention was drawn back to the two old gentlemen.

"You think old Pelias will take it lying back or do you think he still wants to have a finger in the pie?"

"His oldest son, Ram, will have nothing to do with his ambitions. He is only interested in running Lazar. He didn't even come to the pledging of fealty . . . sent his Steward."

I think we will hear from Lorn. He's not used to letting things lie."

"He's a fool and should let well enough alone. His son, Evans, is Governor of Atlan. What else does he want?"

"I think he wants to rule Atlan, even if it costs the life of his son."

"Wonder what the Queen will do? She's still untried and probably has bright ideas to initiate changes. Women always do; can't leave well enough alone."

Bortei, eavesdropping, was trying to keep a straight face. So, they thought Lorn Pelias was still a force to be reckoned with. She had realized somewhat after his imprisonment that even from the tower he could create mischief. His activity would have to be looked into. He still had his voice and probably followers.

Following the banquet, there was dancing. Prince Sinuhe and Jovan led their partners onto the floor. The dance reminded Bortei of a minuet and somehow she seemed to know the steps. Dorcas had been asked, but no one had asked her, so she stood against the wall and watched. As her gaze moved around the room, she saw Manetho come in. When he approached Dorcas, she wondered and was about to cross the floor when a pimply faced young man asked if she would like to dance.

"I'd be delighted," Bortei told him to his utter amazement. He had already steeled himself for a refusal. He led her securely through the dance and when she passed close to Prince Sinuhe, she suspected he had recognized her. His gaze seemed to follow her.

The next dance was a ring-dance. Near its end, she found herself partnered with Prince Jovan. She was surprised when he addressed her by name.

"Lady Rena, are you enjoying yourself?" he asked politely.

"Immensely," she replied, bestowing on him a guarded smile.

"Dorcas said you were a cousin of hers, but I don't recall ever meeting you before."

"I'm one of her poor relations," her accent heavy on the word poor.

He gave a short chuckle, then it was time to hand her on to the next partner.

The next time she noticed Jovan, he was dancing with Dorcas. Before the dance ended, he contrived to be close by. Taking Bortei's arm, he said, "I would like to introduce you to Prince Sinuhe."

Bortei was about to decline when his grip on her arm tightened. She gave him a surprised look and stopped.

"The Lord Manetho has asked for you."

Bortei stiffened and after a moment's hesitation, asked, "Why? . . . Your Highness."

Before he could answer they were approached by Lord Manetho carrying two goblets. "Lady Rena, I hope you are enjoying the festivities." Proffering one of the goblets, he asked, "Would you like to join me in a drink?"

Uncertain of the reason for the request, Bortei frowned but took the chalice. It contained a golden liquid. When Bortei sniffed at the contents, the aroma was of a good vintage wine and she took a tiny sip. The taste was mellow, not tart nor sweet. In compliment, she inclined her head to Lord Manetho. She was somewhat surprised when instead of taking a drink himself, he handed his goblet to Jovan.

"Prince Jovan mentioned that you wanted to talk to me about something? How can I be of service?" Bortei asked Manetho.

"Only that the Lady has been recognized and that she should enjoy the next dance with his Highness Prince Sinuhe."

Bortei took another sip to cover her surprise. She tried to read Manetho's face from under her lashes, wondering why he would disclose who she was. His face was bland, revealing nothing. Suddenly she was assailed by a feeling of apprehension. She looked for Dorcas, wanting to return immediately to her apartment.

"Lady Rena, may I have the next dance?" When Bortei looked up, Prince Sinuhe bowed politely and put his arm around her waist. He took her goblet and handed it to Jovan.

The dance was for couples.

"Lady Rena . . ."

"Oh, knock it off, Evans," Bortei told him curtly. And she wondered to herself why he always rubbed her the wrong way.

There was a chuckle. "Lady Bortei," he whispered into her ear, "We are both victims of a conspiracy."

"What kind of conspiracy?" she asked and stopped.

"Please, continue dancing. We don't want to draw attention."

"I have already drawn notice by dancing with you. Now, what kind of conspiracy are you talking about? Oops! Did I step on your toes?"

"You did." He tilted her head up and searched her eyes, which were beginning to become unfocused. "It's time we get off the dance floor," Sinuhe mumbled to himself and waved to Jovan. "Take her other arm and let's get her out of here," he told him.

Supporting Bortei on the other side, Jovan helped to lead her from the room.

Bortei had no memory for how she made it to the apartment. Tan Rue was there and took her in hand. He undressed her, then gave her a shower. Clean and scented, she lay languidly on the bed finally noticing Sinuhe sitting beside her. He looked down at her and she felt an unaccustomed warmth spread up from her groin and throughout her whole body.

"I guess you are feeling the effects by now," Sinuhe said.

"Effects . . . of what? . . . what's . . . going on?" Bortei said with some effort.

"Well, they thought you would be reluctant, so they sped up our getting to know each other."

"Sinuhe!"

"Don't get mad at me."

"Nor me," Jovan said, kneeling behind her on the bed. She had not noticed him come into the room.

"Come toward me," Sinuhe told her, and gently pulled her forward until she was poised above him.

Both were gentle and slow as they guided her through experiences she never dreamed existed.

Somewhat later, another voice intruded.

"Ariel?" she asked.

"Come, Bortei, come," he said and pulled her toward him. There was a gentle kiss and then a strong arm tucking her under his body.

***

Bortei awakened and sat up. There were three bodies in bed with her. Considering how unthinkable her night had been, she buried her head in her hands, then ran her hands over her scalp. She let out a hiss. No hair! She would never be accustomed to having none.

"Lady Bortei?" a voice whispered. "Can I get you something?"

"Tan Rue? Yes, a glass of water, please."

While she drank the water, a hand moved caressingly up her thigh. When she looked, it was Jovan. He was partly awake and in his half sleep had rolled toward her. As soon as Tan Rue removed the glass, he pulled her into his arms. Their activity awakened the others.

She must have fallen asleep again. When she awoke, Sinuhe's face was close to hers, quietly watching.

She grabbed him by the hair. "Whose mischief was this? I want an answer and I want it now," she told him peremptorily. When he pulled her into his arms, she protested, "Not now. I'm still subject to responses I don't understand. Sinuhe, I want an answer. Why would Lord Manetho hand me a spiked drink?"

"Bortei, may I call you Bortei?"

Her eyes flared and then subsided. With a whimsical grin, she replied, "As long as we are in this unclothed condition and in the same bed."

"Don't you agree that there is a growing attachment after sexual relations? It's supposed to break down barriers."

Bortei looked at him with incredulous eyes." What are you talking about?" She protested when Jovan began pulling her toward him. To quell her objection, he fastened his lips firmly over her mouth.

Sinuhe, with his mouth close to her ear, hurriedly whispered, "Bortei, think. This is an action Lord Manetho would never accede to. This is completely out of character. This must have come down through Master Ashir. Someone else or something else is pulling strings. For sometime, Zennor has suspected some other power, but he is not too sure. We talked about it before he became High-Priest. The last Queen's erratic behavior became suspect. It was as if she were rebelling against something. Don't mention this to anyone, but keep it in mind. Don't trust anyone. We will talk about this some other time. For now, we need to go back to a more normal performance."

He promptly followed suit by running his hand up between her thighs, and she responded immediately by sharply slapping his hand.

Pulling herself up on her elbow, "Now, I want to know what was in that drink?" she demanded.

"Lady Bortei?" Tan Rue answered, instead of Sinuhe, "It contained a depressant to lower your resistance and also something to heighten your sensuality."

"It did do that," Bortei admitted. "And the reason for all this was what Prince Sinuhe postulated? To break down my resistance?"

"Yes, it was believed, that otherwise, your Majesty would not accept a husband and two consorts."

While Bortei sat digesting this, a hand began to fondle her breasts. Bortei took the hand away. "Ariel, be a good boy and keep your hands to yourself. And Sinuhe, would you please move away a bit. Nearness still gets my hormones going. And right now, I'd like to think. And the same thing was given to those three?" she asked Tan Rue.

"Yes, but in a smaller dosage."

"Hmmm, I see," she said as she climbed out of the bed. "Tan Rue, hand me my robe," and turning back to the bed, she said to its occupants, "Gentlemen, this encounter has ended and all are dismissed." To Tan Rue, "I think this requires a long bath," and with her lips quivering, "or maybe a cold shower." The situation discomfited her greatly, but in some skewed way appealed to her sense of humor.

***

When Sinuhe walked into the morning-room, Ariel and Jovan were already sitting at breakfast. Questioningly, he looked down at the fourth setting.

"Lord Manetho will join us for breakfast." Ariel informed him.

Sinuhe had just been seated when Jovan suddenly broke up laughing. "Gentlemen, this encounter has ended and all are dismissed," he mimicked Bortei and the others joined in his laughter.

"We seem to be having a pleasant morning," Manetho said, coming through the door.

All three rose and bowed.

Manetho took his seat and looked around, "What was the amusement concerning?"

Jovan looked at Manetho while his lips quivered. "Her Majesty, the Lady Bortei, dismissed us from her bed by nonchalantly saying, 'Gentlemen, this encounter has ended and all are dismissed'." Again, he fell into cackling.

Manetho, putting marmalade on his toast, was trying to appear serene but could not quite suppress a smile. Looking at Sinuhe, "Her Majesty was not, let's say, offended?"

"No, I would not say offended. It seemed a novel experience for her." Sinuhe said slowly, letting his fork rest on his plate. "But she was not at ease with us being there together. I think she was slightly embarrassed. But most of all, I think she was disquieted by her own responses."

Manetho, looking at him, asked "And you?"

Sinuhe shrugged. "She is a woman."

"I see," Manetho said, and there was a slight hint of sadness to his voice as he contemplated them. "Can you three work with her? Or more to the point, are you willing to work with her?

"For the future of Atlan, yes," Sinuhe replied, and the others nodded in agreement.

"Now," Manetho said briskly, "she has requested a statement on the status of the country. She wishes to be briefed and I think she wants to be briefed in depth."

"She won't be pleased to hear about the condition Atlan is in with its warring factions. Or the state of its finances, either. I'm afraid we will have to raise taxes to cover expenses. The last Queen left us a h . . . a mess," Sinuhe finished.

Manetho looked at Ariel.

"We have no money to pay our soldiers. Especially the mercenaries, who will rebel if they are not paid soon," Ariel said.

"The provinces swore their alliance to the Queen."

"Lord Manetho, you know how long that will last," Sinuhe said bitterly. "And my father is still fermenting dissention. I don't know how she will react when she learns the condition of her country."

"My advice to you gentlemen is to be open and honest. I don't think she will tolerate deceptions. So, when you brief her, give her the whole picture. Today, she will be moving into her new apartment. You will find things there you won't understand, technology we supposedly have not yet discovered. I'm only telling you this so you will not be alarmed. Most of the things you don't understand, don't touch. They can deliver a nasty surprise."

CHAPTER EIGHT

Bortei stepped through the bathroom door and told Tan Rue, "Ask Dorcas to share my breakfast. And tell her she need not hurry."

Tan Rue gave her a quick look, wondering what she was up to again. Nearly everything she initiated involved a surprise or two.

When he was out of the room, Bortei kneeled down to inspect the water spouts. So close, she could smell a wood fire. Ah, she thought, the water is heated in the next room with a wood burning boiler. She had often wondered where the hot water came from. Primitive, she thought and shrugged. The apartment she had briefly shared with Minyar was more on par with the technology she was familiar with. Here, there were contradictions.

A cough caused her to turn. Tan Rue stood behind her and had been watching. "Just curious," she said with a toothy grin and rose.

After a leisurely bath, she dressed comfortably in what she called her at-home clothes. When she entered the dining room, Dorcas was already waiting. She almost laughed at the curious look Dorcas gave her attire.

"Believe me, these are very comfortable," Bortei explained. She pointed to a chair. "Come and sit. Let's have breakfast."

After Bortei was seated, Dorcas poured Bortei's breakfast drink, but when she started to butter her buns, Bortei protested, "Dorcas, you butter your own buns and leave mine alone."

Somewhat flustered, Dorcas sat down.

"Good, now let's start. What kind of jelly do you like?"

"Lady Bortei . . ."

"I understand, now let's eat. Hand me that knife." After biting into her bread, she reached for a piece of fruit and pared it with the knife. "Dorcas, you need to learn to act natural around me. I can't stand that bowing and bobbing. Do you want some tea?" Bortei asked. "Good, give me your cup."

To Dorcas's consternation, it was Bortei who waited on her.

"Ahem," Manetho coughed. "Lady Bortei, you wished to see me?"

When Dorcas saw Manetho, she jumped up from her chair and bowed.

"Dorcas, sit down and finish your breakfast and quit bobbing," Bortei said, irritated. "Manetho, please be seated. I surmise you had breakfast already."

He gave her an amused look. "Yes, my Lady, I'm well fortified."

"As you know, I have asked the Consorts to give me a briefing. To receive a briefing, one needs to have pertinent questions. As my counselor, it is your job to supply me with appropriate queries."

Seeing that Dorcas had hurriedly finished her breakfast, she smiled and said, "Thank you for joining me. Manetho and I have several items to discuss. I will visit with you later, and remember when you leave, don't bob, just walk out."

After the door closed behind Dorcas, Manetho asked, "What are your current concerns?"

"Everything. As you know, I was thrown into this mess without prior consultation. I need to know what Atlan is, how it is functioning and its present state of affairs. And one more thing, then I will drop it. Lord Manetho," she said severely, "I trusted you when I took the challis. I will not ever be drugged again."

"It was only done to break the ice," Manetho explained with a rueful smile.

"That was not an ice breaker; it was an ice crusher. Now back to Atlan. What can you tell me about its current affairs of state?"

"Atlan is broke. It had been torn by constant warfare among the provinces, each jostling for more power, or to add more land to their holdings."

Bortei digested this for a moment. "What you are telling me, then, is Atlan is in one hell of a mess. Tell the Consorts I want a financial statement, broken down into its expenditures. What about the state of the military, if there is one? Well . . . what I'm thinking of will probably have to wait. I would like for them to consider a dossier on those provincial governors and what makes them think they can govern."

"The same as you asked of Prince Sinuhe?"

Bortei gave him an amused look. "Yes, precisely. What do you think of it?"

"It could be informative."

"Your remark is noncommittal. My idea is that the job should not be inherited, but given to those best qualified, someone with experience and education. But I guess some of the changes will have to wait."

"I will convey your wishes to the Consorts. Also, your apartment is now ready. Would you like to view it?"

"It is? Wonderful! Let's go and look it over."

Bortei rose and Manetho followed.

"Your audience chamber and governmental offices will remain where they are now, as well as the office of your adjutant, Tan T'Sien. Your private office and apartment will be connected by this long hallway," he explained as they walked briskly down a windowless corridor.

When he opened the first door, Bortei let out a cry of pleasure. "Windows!" she exclaimed and walked toward them. She looked out onto a lawn bordered with shrubs and flowers. "Believe it or not, I feel I can breathe in here," she told Manetho. In the next room, her eyes immediately fell on a familiar contraption. "A computer?" she asked, astonished. "What is it tied into?"

"For the time being, it is only your personal computer tied into its companion on Tan T'Sien's desk. He has already written programs so you can use it now."

"I have noticed a huge contradiction here. The former Queen's apartment is antiquated. There are no modern conveniences, or technologies. I love candlelight, but only in romantic settings and I don't like the smoky torches. But here, you have electricity, a computer, and I hope modern bathroom facilities."

"Through natural disturbances and wars, Atlan has slipped back into what you would call the dark ages. But some of the knowledge of our former technology has survived, but are not workable on a large scale." Walking to the door behind her, he opened it and asked, "Would you like to see the rest of your apartment?"

"Lead on."

Next was her living room. She noted it was furnished in pastels. There were three couches forming a rectangle, an easy-chair placed along a wall with a free standing lamp and a side table. There were no paintings on the wall. But they could come later, Bortei thought. There were bookshelves, alas still empty, along one of the walls. She found herself standing before huge patio doors leading outside onto a terrace. Beyond that, was a garden with bordered walkways and some distance further in a group of trees, she could see a gazebo. Nearer the house in view of the living room was a swimming pool.

"Your bedroom is in here," Manetho said, opening the door.

When Bortei stepped through the door, she immediately liked the room. There was a huge bed, a vanity with a three-sided mirror, a large wardrobe and a chaise-lounge situated in front of another patio door to give her a view of the outside world while she reclined comfortably. Her bathroom had a private room with a toilet, a huge improvement on the privacy screen.

"Is it to your liking?" Manetho asked.

She gave him a bright smile and told him, "Much better. I can most definitely live here."

"Then I will leave your Majesty to enjoy her apartment. By this evening, I will have questions prepared for you to ask the Consorts."

"Thank you, Manetho."

As soon as he departed, she ventured outside to investigate her garden. It was larger than she had first thought. It continued to the foot of the mountain behind the Palace, and when she clambered up a small butte, to her surprise she could see into a familiar enclosure she had stayed in with Minyar.

Back in the apartment, she opened drawers and her wardrobe. Adjacent to her living room was a small workroom with a console. Ah, a small office for me, she thought. There was another room, round and empty, painted in unrelieved white. When she went outside, she could see that it was a donjon forming the corner wall of her garden.

Back inside, Bortei began to wander restlessly from room to room, then decided to go to her official office. When she arrived, in the middle of her otherwise empty desk, lay a portfolio. She sat down in the chair and opened it.

"Oh, my goodness!" she exclaimed. It was the dossier she had requested from Prince Sinuhe. She began reading it and started to chuckle. Scratching her head, she thought, I bet this is called revenge. The entire dossier was written in an elaborate style with long, intricate sentences. Patiently, she read through it, making notes as she worked.

"There you are!" came an unguarded exclamation from Tan Rue. "I'm sorry, Lady Bortei."

"It's all right. What is it you want?"

"Only to ask if you would like some refreshments?"

"How late it is?"

"It's almost six o'clock."

"Lord Manetho hasn't come back yet?"

"No, Lady Bortei."

"Something to eat would be a good idea," she told Tan Rue.

She had been so engrossed in reading, time had gone by quickly. According to the dossier, Sinuhe was more than qualified to govern Atlan. His education was broad based. Chewing the inside of her cheek, she contemplated what that would mean to her.

The door opened and Tan Rue announced, "The Lord Manetho, my Lady."

Manetho came through the door as Bortei rose. "Manetho," she said, inclining her head.

After a short bow, he said, "My Lady, here are the questions I have prepared."

"Thank you, would you join me for a repast?"

He handed her a small portfolio and with a short bow said, "I thank you for the kind offer, but I have promised the Consorts assistance in their preparation for tomorrow's briefing."

Bortei took the portfolio. "I appreciate your help and I will see you tomorrow, at nine o'clock."

After the door was closed, she rose and gathered up Sinuhe's dossier and the questionnaires. She went back to her apartment and into her small office. She put both folders on the desk and went in search of Tan Rue.

She crossed the hallway and there was a door she had not seen before. It led into a dining room where a swinging door was still in motion. Pushing through it, she was reminded of a butler's pantry. At its end was a baize door. Curious, she opened it and walked into a kitchen that, even by her standards, was quite modern.

There was a shocked exclamation from two young girls standing stiffly at a worktable.

"It's all right," Bortei assured them. "I'm only looking for Tan Rue."

"Lady Bortei!" Dana exclaimed, as she came into the kitchen. "You shouldn't be here."

"Why not, my dear?" Bortei asked, amused.

"You're the Queen."

"I know. But that doesn't make the kitchen forbidden territory. When I come in here, or any other place you

89

work, I'm invisible. Only answer when I ask. And no bowing and bobbing around," she added severely. "It makes me dizzy."

When Tan Rue came back into the kitchen, he informed her, "I have set out refreshments for you in the dining room."

"The kitchen would have been good enough," Bortei told him with a broad grin.

***

Light filtered through the curtains, and the outline of the room became visible. The furniture was different. It took a second for Bortei to remember that she was now in her own apartment and not in the former Queen's.

She sat up in bed. No Tan Rue, she thought, and slid out from under the covers. Barefoot, she padded to the huge glass door and looked out. Two moons were high in the sky. No wonder there was so much light.

She went to her office and turned on the electric lights. What a delightful difference from candles, she thought, and went to the desk. On top was the dossier Sinuhe had written and also an outline of the questions she was going to ask today. But all this could wait. She went into the donjon's ground room. Yesterday, she had confiscated several small carpets and stacked them on the west side of the room. She sat down facing east and went into meditation.

Maybe ten minutes had passed or possibly an hour, Bortei thought, unworried, as she came out of her meditation feeling alert and refreshed. Then she went through her martial art forms, not so easy, since her muscles were no longer used to the exertion. Afterward, she returned to her private office realizing, lo and behold, Tan Rue stood at the door waiting for her.

"Good morning, Tan Rue. Did you sleep well?"

"Thank you, my Lady, very well. Would you like to have your bath?"

Pulling her nightshirt away from her body, she agreed, "I think it would be a good idea." Despite holding her exercise to the minimum, it had raised sweat on her body. "What time is it?"

"It is about seven-thirty."

"I will have a bath and breakfast, and by then, I will need to get ready for the nine o'clock briefing."

***

Bortei walked into the briefing room, somber, with Lord Manetho and her adjutant two paces behind. Because of the presence of the Consorts' top advisors, she was dressed in ceremonial garb and heavily made up.

She immediately noticed the Consorts' indirect gazes scanning her face, but her eyes moved over them in detached contemplation. Her deportment gave no hint of a memory of the intimate event of the other night. She was perfectly composed as she took her seat at the head of the table.

"Gentlemen, be seated." Turning to Price Sinuhe, "Your Highness, you may proceed."

"Your Majesty, we have only begun to sort out the condition Atlan is in. The last war with Bagoas, the kingdom to our south, has cost us dearly in men and money. Madam, the coffers are empty. We thought to raise taxes, but the people are already overburdened and could riot."

From her consultation with Lord Manetho, she knew the subject would be raised. She had thought about it for some time before joining this meeting. She reconsidered it only for a moment before she asked, "When was the last time taxes were collected?"

"Nine months ago."

"Nevertheless, it must be done again. I have considered for a limited time only to raise them thirty percent, which is a reduction from the present taxation, until the coffers show some assets. Then all tax laws are rescinded and I want any and all loopholes closed. The new tax law will be thirty percent of gross income. When can it be initiated?"

"But Madame some people would pay exorbitant taxes . . ."

"What the Minister of Finance, Lord Seaton, would like to say is, that it would not find favor in certain places," Lord Manetho said dryly.

"Thirty percent for three month," she reiterated. When she turned to Ariel, he responded with, "Your Majesty, I have to report that the Army is broke and I'm afraid the Mercenaries will demand to be paid."

"Like last time, we could borrow from the Governor of Lazar . . ."

"And what usury fee would he charge?" Bortei interrupted Lord Seaton.

"The last time it was twenty-six percent," Prince Sinuhe said.

"Lord Seaton, no wonder we are broke. I have also heard that Lord Lorn has yet to cease his meddling. Prince Ariel, can we expect trouble from those quarters?"

"Yes, Lady Bortei."

"How soon?"

"Probably this year. We are keeping a close watch on this situation. Naturally, Lord Lorn has money," Prince Ariel said cynically. "Lazar is one of the richest provinces of Atlan, next to the Rimal Mountains."

"Will Lord Uster side with Lazar?" General Doren asked.

"There is no love lost between the two."

Bortei gave a gentle cough to bring the attention back to her. "Gentlemen, we still have finances to discuss. Now, I would like to see the collected taxes and a breakdown of the taxed income and expenditure. I want to know to what department the money went and how much. We have a blackboard in this room." She handed Tan T'Sien two sheets of paper, "Please write these figures down and then those indicated by Lord Seaton."

Tan T'Sien rose from his chair behind Bortei's seat and went to the black board. Poised, holding a chalk, he waited for Lord Seaton to call out the numbers from his notes. He then added the numbers from the sheets Bortei had given him.

It didn't take long for Bortei to add the figures up on a small calculator she held concealed in her lap.

Soon the columns mounted on the debit side. When Bortei finished calculating, she handed the results to Tan T'Sien to put on the blackboard. It quickly became apparent that huge sums of money were missing. Lord Seaton's face became ashen white.

"Lord Seaton," Bortei said calmly, "Would you please explain the discrepancy?"

"Your Majesty, I can't explain it. My records don't show this much variance.

"Prince Sinuhe, do your accounts show the same numbers as Lord Seaton's?"

"No, Lady Bortei, they do not. They are more in accord with your findings."

"Have you traced the discrepancy?"

"Yes. I have already traced it to the office of Lord Seaton."

"And in your estimate, Prince Sinuhe?"

"He has skimmed allocation from various departments and very likely lined his own pockets with the money. It will be investigated."

Bortei's face tightened. "Yes, it is very apparent. Prince Ariel, you mentioned that you had no money to pay off the Mercenaries?"

"Yes. The military allotments are all used up."

"Prince Ariel, you will tell your soldiers to take over the house of Lord Seaton. He is to pay the salaries they so richly deserve. If there is not enough money for them, then auction off his properties. Lord Seaton, you are dismissed. If I should hear anything about you or see your face anywhere, I will not hesitate to hand down a death sentence. Prince Ariel, have the order go out this instant."

There was a shocked silence in the room and every eye was on Bortei. The pronouncement had been startling and unexpected.

Prince Ariel sat motionless, then rose. There was a hard look on his face as he exited to give the order to lay siege to the house of Lord Seaton.

Lord Seaton seemed frozen, his face haggard. He stumbled like a blind man as he rose from his seat. He staggered from the room without a look back.

Bortei, pale under the heavy makeup, was shaken. It was not in her nature to be ruthless, but there was a deep seated anger at injustice and dishonesty.

After a protracted silence, Bortei roused herself. "Gentlemen, I think we will call it a day. Prince Sinuhe, you will accompany me. My private office," she told Tan Rue who had miraculously appeared at her side.

She left the conference room and made the walk to her office in silence. When she entered, her desk was still bare except for the dossier from Prince Sinuhe. She walked to her desk and stopped in front of it.

"Prince Sinuhe, you will have the different departments write a summary of their functions and provide a breakdown of their expenditures. I want the reports to be concise and as accurate." Picking up the dossier, she added, "I liked your autobiography; it made long but interesting reading," she told him dryly. "Also, all outgoing reports go through my desk first." She nodded to dismiss him.

Bortei sat down at the desk. She was exhausted. The whole morning had been appalling.

"Lady Bortei?"

"Yes, Tan Rue."

"It's a warm sunny day and since it is past lunchtime, I have taken the liberty to set a table out on the patio."

"Thank you, Tan Rue, I appreciate it."

***

The next morning Bortei dispensed with a briefing and when she entered her official office, she stopped at the threshold and began to laugh. Her desk was piled with paper. Leafing through the files, she found many of them to be petitions. Others, directives to the finance office to clear matters up.

"Tan T'Sien."

There was a rustling of papers and a scraping of a chair. Coming to the door, he asked, "Lady Bortei?"

"Have someone go through these files and separate the spurious ones from the genuine article. Before anything comes to my desk, sort things out and give me a short synopsis of the content."

"Yes, my Lady. I think this will be a better arrangement," Tan T'Sien agreed.

Not able to find anything to do, Bortei went back to her apartment where she ran into Dana making her bed.

She watched the girl for a second. "I surmise you have more clothes now since we first met?"

"Yes, my Lady. Thank you, my Lady."

Bortei waved her off. "How about letting me borrow a dress of yours?"

Dana stared at her.

"Dana, if I go dressed like I am, everyone will gawk at me." Bortei wore clothes she herself designed. "And if I go in my ceremonial garb, they would know who I am. You can see that, don't you?"

"Yes, my Lady," Dana said, her mind racing furiously. Tan Rue was gone and she didn't know if the Queen really could go out without an escort. She could endanger her life.

"Come, Dana, quit stalling. The dress has to be simple. Like a servant's," and as she said it, she shooed Dana out of the room.

In the mean time, Bortei divested herself of the dress she was wearing. Dana took long enough for Bortei to suspect she had been looking for Tan Rue.

Once clothed in a simple dress with her head covered by an artfully arranged scarf, Bortei walked out of the suite through the servants' entrance. She was headed down a corridor she hoped was an exit. Unfortunately, the corridor she had chosen led back into the Palace toward the vicinity of the public area.

Darn, that's not the way I wanted to go, she groused. Rounding the corner of another corridor she came upon a long line of people. The line was segregated into the richly attired and the poor. In Bortei's memory, the hall led into an audience chamber. As she watched, the richly attired line moved quickly and the line of the poor not at all. There was a woman with several small children. Their clothes were in tatters, but clean, and she was crying.

Bortei went to her and sitting beside her on the floor asked, "What's your name?"

"Senta Paar."

"What is it you're seeking?"

There was a deep sigh and renewed tears. "My husband, I tried to get them to release my husband. He was accused of stealing. But he didn't do it. The young Lady, so not to get into trouble, said that my husband stole it. But he didn't."

"Had someone seen her taking whatever she took?"

"Yes, the butler. But no one will listen to him. The young lady insists that my husband stole it and she won't withdraw her accusation. And now I too am out of work. They will put him into a workhouse and the kids and I won't ever see him again. They never come out. They die."

Bortei rubbed her chin. "What's your husband's name?"

"Linus."

Bortei patted the woman's arm, then rose. She walked up to the clerk sitting at a table that blocked access to the room. She searched the table for a piece of paper and found one, then she snapped her fingers, "Please, hand me that pencil," she demanded.

Completely caught off guard, he handed her the requested item. When Bortei turned to go, someone blocked her way. Looking closer at the individual, she recognized Tan Rue without his habit.

"Oh! Incognito," she whispered. "Since you are here, you can get me the name and address of the woman I have been talking to."

Staying within the act, he dared to ask, "And what are you going to do?"

"Go in there to see what's going on."

"That should be enlightening," he murmured.

When the next name was called, Bortei followed the handsomely clad gentleman into the audience chamber. He bowed to the Judge who sat robed on the bench.

"Your Honor, thank you for hearing my petition. As you can see from the deposition, I'm innocent, and my lawyers have been asking for the charge to be dismissed."

"Yes, I know. Naturally the accusation is spurious and we see no reason why you were brought before my court. It clearly is the servant's fault. You can never trust females and their seductive wiles."

"Thank you, Your Honor. There will be a reward coming your way."

Bortei could feel her temper rise as she listened to this deceitful display and the total disregard for justice. Becoming aware of Bortei, the judge asked, "Is this the wench?" and pointed toward her.

The man turned around and gave Bortei a surprised look. "No, Your Honor, I have never seen her before."

"What are you doing in my courtroom?" the Judge snapped.

"I have been here all morning and no one called my name."

"What's your name?"

"Senta Paar. My husband has been falsely accused of taking some valuables from his employer's house. But he didn't do it. The butler saw who did it."

The Judge shook his head. "Likely excuse; now get out of my court," he shouted at her.

Bortei backed to the door and exited. Tan Rue was waiting for her on the other side.

"I want the name of this judge," she told him.

"I know who he is."

"Do you know where he lives?"

"Yes."

"Good. I want to go there."

When they passed Senta Paar, Bortei bent down to her. "Go home. Soon someone will contact you."

The Judge's house turned out to be a magnificent mansion with a well-kept lawn and steps leading up to a pillared front door.

Bortei used the knocker. The door was opened by a liveried servant.

"Servants use the back door," she was told in no uncertain terms.

"Yes, of course. But I just came from Judge . . . ?" Turning to Tan Rue, "Brant," he supplied. "And his courtroom, and I want to see his house," she continued.

Without further ado, Bortei pushed past the servant.

The house was lavish, but tastefully furnished. The furniture, Bortei thought, might be period pieces. There were numerous paintings on the walls and what appeared to be expensive carpets on the floors.

Alarmed by Bortei's manners, the servant had gone to fetch the Lady of the house. They met her coming down the stairs.

The Lady stiffened, squaring her shoulders. Her face angered when she saw Bortei. "Who are you? What is the meaning of you breaking into my house?" she asked imperiously.

"I surmise you're Lady Brant?"

"Yes, I'm the wife of Judge Brant."

"Does he only have this house or does he have others?"

"We have a house out in the country. Why?"

"Good." Bortei said and she and Tan Rue left the house.

"With all due respect. What was all that about?" Tan Rue asked.

"Let's go home. I need to talk to Master Ashir."

***

Bortei was pacing in her official office, formulating in her mind how to pose what she wanted to ask Master Ashir. Expecting the door to open, she was still startled when it did.

"Master Ashir," she said and bowed in respect.

"Lady Bortei."

"Please forgive me for calling on you, but I need to discuss a matter that has arisen. I need a place to stash people, something like a monastery, maybe. A place that is not easily accessible, nor pleasant to live in. Let me tell you what happened this morning."

She commenced to tell Master Ashir about Senta Paar. She was halfway through when Lord Manetho entered, his demeanor agitated.

"Master Ashir, I . . ."

Master Ashir raised his hand to silence him and told Bortei to continue.

She finished her story, then said, "As you see, I cannot in all good conscience have this Judge practice law. A slap on the wrist is not enough. Even if I have him disbarred, he will still have his ill-gained riches and his mind to start another career. I'm also concerned about Lorn Pelias. Even from the tower, he is still stirring up trouble. I threatened him once, that if he didn't behave I would have him scrub kitchen pots for the rest of his life. He could only do that if he was confined to a monastery. Just imagine how many pots and pans they have."

"When you talk of a monastery, are you implying a religious order?"

"Well . . . is there any other kind?"

"Yes. There is an order of men who live together in a place of utter isolation in an icy waste up in the arctic region. Will that do for you?"

"Hmmm," she said and rubbed her chin. "And they will tolerate those miscreants among them?"

"They wouldn't be too disturbed by them. Not only do they live in isolation, but are also solitary, only interacting when necessary."

"Strange group of people," Bortei mused. "That would work," she told Master Ashir. "Do they have to be notified or can we just drop them in?"

"I will arrange it." Master Ashir bowed and left the room.

"Lady Bortei!" Lord Manetho exclaimed, "You don't just summon Master Ashir. If you have a problem, I'm here to help you."

"Lord Manetho, when I have a problem, I ask God directly; I don't need a priest to intercede for me."

Speechless, Lord Manetho only stared at her.

"Now, I need to talk to Prince Sinuhe."

***

"Lady Bortei?"

She pushed the map she was reading aside. "Sinuhe." Pointing to the chair in front of her desk, she said, "Please sit down. A matter has arisen on which I need you to act."

"The Judge Brant matter?"

"Then Lord Manetho has talked to you?"

There was a short chuckle. "Yes, my Lady, he did."

"I want all his assets up for auction, and his properties, except for the house in the country, sold. Naturally, I want him disbarred. Then, there is the matter of the Paar family. I think the woman and her husband can earn some money by preparing the Judge's possessions for the auction. Then a place of employment will have to be found for them. Oh, yes. The case against the husband is to be dismissed."

"Judge Brant? Do you want him summarily dismissed or through due process?"

"Oh, we would not deprive his Honor of his day in court," Bortei said sarcastically. "Why have you not done anything about him?"

"He has not come to my attention."

"How long have I been Queen, three . . . four months?"

"Half a year, my Lady."

"That long?" After a momentary silence, "Pretty soon you will need to seek a replacement for him. Will that be difficult?"

"Yes. It is a very coveted position."

"Sorry, I can't help you there. But I want dossiers from your narrowed down selection."

"Short and sweet?"

Bortei chuckled. "Yes. I don't like all that reading and I don't like Tan T'Sien wasting his time wading through all that paperwork."

"I'm sorry about my autobiography, but . . ."

"Sinuhe, I asked for it. We got off on the wrong foot. Like I said, you govern; I rule. I want to be informed. I want to know what's going on . . . kept on top of things. We can both have our way if we work together. Despotism doesn't work. Then, there is your father."

"Like Ariel said, he is keeping an eye on him. He still has a following and he is still working to overthrow the present Queen," Sinuhe said with a short bow to Bortei.

For a moment she glared at him. "And you?"

Sinuhe's smile was very slight as he decided to be blunt. "Would you like the whole pie, or only a small slice?"

Her face tightened, almost imperceptibly. "That depends on how greedy I should be."

He looked startled for a moment. "I stand corrected."

"I will have a briefing two days from now. This should give you enough time to prepare."

He rose and bowed. "Thank you, Lady Bortei."

As he left, Bortei thought, ouch! He is still smarting.

Chapter Nine

It didn't take long for Lorn Pelias to make himself felt, trying to ferment a revolution. His rallying cry was *Atlan for the Atlantes*. His aim was to destabilize the government and then use outright force. Four weeks after he had been confined to the tower, troops came marching into Pathean.

Bortei was reading the first of the dossiers from seven of the provinces; Lazar was the one exception. Prince Sinuhe walked into her office.

"Lady Bortei."

"Yes, your Highness."

The formality usually amused him, but today there was a mirthless smile on his lips. "My father has sent his troops into Pathean. Ariel has gone out to meet them."

"How many troops does your father have and what kind?"

"About three hundred, trained in warfare. They are mostly mercenaries who have left us to join him. He at least has money to pay them."

"And Ariel?"

"The border towns have armed themselves and joined Ariel. We only have about one hundred trained soldiers."

"That doesn't sound promising."

"No, Lady Bortei."

"Then we have to think of something besides combat." Looking at Sinuhe's uncomprehending look, "We need to be practical. There are not enough troops and we cannot sustain a long conflict. Now leave me, I have some thinking to do."

After Sinuhe closed the door, Bortei sat back in her chair and began to contemplate the situation. *I should have taken Lorn Pelias out instead of giving him a chance for mischief. First of all, I need to know what's going on. I wonder if the Silent Brothers could transport me to the battle scene.* She was not very surprised at how they appeared and disappeared. It was simply a case of raising and lowering their vibration. Her martial arts instructor had explained it to her some time ago.

"Yes, this is how it is done, Lady Bortei." Master Ashir materialized in front of her.

"Master Ashir, I could use your counsel."

"Something occurred to you?"

Bortei chuckled. "There's an old joke on my home world. But I figure that as outrageous as it sounds, it could work. How about a war no one goes to?"

"And what makes you think any such thing could transpire?"

"Master Ashir, first I beg your indulgence. To test whether my idea is workable, I need to know what's happening. I need to be on the scene. I will likely need considerable help, possibly from some of the monks who have medical knowledge. I need someone who can act as quickly as the Silent Ones. I guess what I'm trying to tell you is that I need to play it by ear."

"You have my assistance." Master Ashir replied, taking a great liking to this unconventional woman. He had decided to help her in any way he could. Even disregarding orders from the Hidden Ones, whoever they were.

"Thank you, Master Ashir. Tan Rue," she called.

When he entered, he could barely suppress a stare when he saw Master Ashir in the room with her.

"Tan Rue, I need one of those outfits you wear," she told him. Tan Rue's expression was one of incredulity that made even Master Ashir chuckle.

When one of the Silent Ones appeared in the room with a habit on his arm, Tan Rue almost blanched. "She doesn't mean any disrespect," Tan Rue whispered hoarsely. He had begun to appreciate this unpredictable and unorthodox Queen.

"None taken," Master Ashir assured him.

Bortei got the impression that Master Ashir was enjoying all this.

After Bortei was dressed in the habit, she disappeared from the room to reappear on top of a small mountain. Below her was a valley where a very one-sided battle was raging.

Her troops were losing.

She breathed harshly as she scanned the landscape. The backdrop of the valley was another mountain, higher than the one she was standing on. I wish I had field glasses, she thought and in that instant was handed a pair. She gave her silent companion an astonished look. "Almost like having a genie," she mumbled.

She trained the glasses on the slope of the taller mountain. There was a huge field of boulders, probably left over from an ancient glacier. She wondered if there was a way to loosen them. Suddenly there was a loud rumble and the mountainside started to come down. She gave her companion a horrified look. "God," she said, and swallowed hard. She had goose-bumps all over her body and trembled. Looking down below, friend and foe were scrambling to get away from the avalanche.

Her next thought was the field hospital and she appeared there instantly. When she looked for her companion, he had disappeared.

She saw seven monks from Tan Rue's order and a few hospital personnel sitting on benches. When she had appeared, one of the monks had come toward her. He had been told to support her in any way, without question.

"We were told to assist you," he told Bortei.

"Can we appropriate horses?"

"Yes. We brought several with us."

"Good. Let's go."

Eight tethered mounts stood beneath the shade of several trees.

They rode away to the bewilderment of the hospital personnel. It all had transpired so quickly, no one had a chance to respond. After only about a mile, they met up with the first casualties coming toward them. They were her troops with a horse drawn wagon carrying the wounded. Bortei and her detachment dismounted and the monks hurried to give first aid.

Bortei looked for the ranking soldier. It was one of the mercenaries. He was slightly wounded.

"What's your name and where is your commander?" Bortei asked him.

He gave Bortei an incongruous look. She was clearly a woman wearing a monk's habit. "I'm Sergeant Sardis, in the service of the Queen. My commander is Colonel Riva. He has also been wounded but stayed back to rally the men."

"Thank you, Sergeant Sardis; there is a field hospital not quite a mile to the west."

Bortei turned around and as she did her eyes fell on a donkey whose owner was having trouble controlling it.

She rode up to him. "Soldier, would you mind exchanging your donkey for my horse?"

"You must be kidding lady. This stupid thing won't do what he's told. My horse was shot out from under me. To keep up with the wagon, I caught this ass. He has been nothing but trouble."

"All right, your donkey for my horse."

"By all means, you can have him," and he dismounted.

Bortei slid off her horse and slowly approached the donkey. She extended her hand toward him and stroked his muzzle. "Now, you're going to be a good boy and I'm going to ride you." She took the reins from the soldier, stepped up beside the donkey and mounted him. She patted his neck and gave him an encouraging slap on the rump. Reluctantly, the donkey moved forward one foot at a time. "We won't get anywhere like this, buddy," she told him. Something told her not to kick his flanks.

"Where is the battle field?" Bortei asked silently.

As if in answer, her donkey turned south and picked up speed.

Well, well, well, Bortei thought, sending out her mind. You must know something about recalcitrant donkeys, and she grinned.

He had trotted along for half an hour when they came over a rise. Below was a valley and troops were arranged on both sides ready for battle.

Now, I could use a voice amplifier, Bortei thought.

A hand appeared and one was affixed to her habit.

Taken aback she mumbled, "Wonders never cease."

Bortei urged the donkey down the slope. When she arrived at its bottom, one side suddenly shouted, "For the Queen," and the other, "for Atlan." And into the ensuing pause, with her voice amplified, Bortei could be heard shouting, "Aw come on guys, will you just for once knock it off."

There was dead silence, all heads turned toward her. All they saw was a figure in a monk's habit riding toward them on a donkey. The donkey was so small that the rider's feet almost dragged the ground.

There was a small knoll and she headed for it. As soon as she stopped, her donkey started to relieve himself.

"Agh!" Bortei exclaimed and pulled her feet up. She looked down and then out at the troops. "Wouldn't you say, he's stealing the show?" she asked them and then began to laugh.

There were some chuckles and then everyone began to laugh outright.

When it was quiet again, Bortei's voice rang out. "I'm Bortei, by the grace of the Oracle, Queen of Atlan. I didn't ask to be your Queen, it was thrust upon me. Believe me, I can imagine spending my days in a more pleasant occupation. But here I am. The kind of Atlan you envision can only be achieved through cooperation and not through strife. Wars destroy, cooperation builds. We want to build Atlan, not destroy it. What I ask of you is your participation in building this dream into reality. I can only do this if you work with me."

Bortei urged her donkey further down the knoll and was met by Prince Ariel who dismounted and helped her up onto his horse. The donkey stripped of his saddle and bridle, ambled away, nibbling at the grass.

Ariel led the horse up to a man who was sitting all by himself on a piebald gelding, all decked out in armor.

When Bortei came closer, she recognized Lorn Pelias, Lord of Lazar.

"What have we here?" Bortei's voice could be heard saying, "Our royal pain in the butt and trouble maker, Lorn Pelias. Have I not told you to remain in your tower?" She turned to the troops. "He wants to rule Atlan, knowing that if anything happens to me, his younger brother, his son, and his nephews would be instantly killed. His ambition is to rule Atlan and rule it to suit himself. He is not concerned with your lives. Why don't you go home to your wives and children? Go run your businesses and better the circumstances you live in."

"Do not listen to her," Lorn Pelias called out. "She is only trying to lull you into compliance with her talk of the Oracle. It's just a bunch of lies . . ."

"Lorn Pelias," Bortei interrupted sternly. "I will remind you of what I promised. If you trouble Atlan again, you will for the rest of your life scrape out pots and pans. And so it will be."

Suddenly two hooded figures appeared beside Lorn Pelias's horse and he was lifted off and disappeared. Sounds of fear moved through the assembled crowd and then there was silence.

Into the stillness, Bortei said, "Go to the west. There is a tent set up. There is food and drink and if you are wounded, you can receive attention for that, as well."

Ariel swung up behind her and they rode off toward Azzan.

***

"That wasn't a bad speech," Ariel commented.

"I'm glad you agree. I meant every word of it."

"I'm sorry; I didn't mean to be flippant."

Suddenly Bortei started to laugh. "That damned donkey. I couldn't have created a better tension breaker."

The two rode for a while, both chuckling.

"How are you doing?"

Because Bortei could hear real concern in his voice, she answered him truthfully. "Hell, I don't know. I wasn't raised or educated to be a Queen. I ran an estate. I know how to deal with people. I learned that being as honest as possible is the best way to get their cooperation."

"You have mine."

"Thank you; I really appreciate it. I hate working against opposition. It wears you down and leads to nothing. Like I said, cooperation is the only way to go."

It was much less hot than it had been out on the battlefield. Clouds were coming up from the west. Maybe it would rain. The terrain was becoming hilly and the horse, carrying two riders, was tiring. Bortei and Ariel dismounted.

"There's a small lake behind that hill," Ariel pointed out. "We can let the horse rest and cool off."

It only took a short while and they walked into the woods, and through the trees they saw the sun sparkle off the water. It looked cool and inviting. Although only wearing a monk's habit, Bortei was perspiring. Ariel, wearing battle-gear, had sweat running down his face.

After unsaddling the horse and hobbling his front legs, both divested themselves of their clothes and waded into the water, then dove under.

"Feels good," Ariel said, having surfaced behind her.

Bortei, without answering him, dove again and swam further away from him. But as she broke surface, he was beside her.

"Are you playing at being the pursuer?"

"Bortei, I'm just a poor old soldier who, instead of having a loving wife to return home to, has to play consort to a Queen."

"That bad, huh?"

"You're laughing at me," he accused her.

"Well . . ." she said and dove again.

This time he came up in front of her. They rolled and played; she at swimming away and he at being the pursuer.

After a while, they surfaced together and he kissed her.

"You know, there are fish down there," she told him, pointing down.

"Don't change the subject; we are not going fishing."

Bortei grabbed his hair with both hands and pulled his head toward her. She kissed him.

After they waded out of the water, he asked, "Do you mind if the blanket smells like horse?"

"I could imagine worse smells." She ran away, but let him catch her.

The sun had moved farther to the west and a cool wind rustled the leaves of the trees. Bortei, giving Ariel one last kiss, rose.

"Now a warm place and a hot meal would be nice," she told him, as she pulled the habit over her head.

"There is a small village not far from here, about three miles or so."

"And we just walk in with our getup?"

"That would cause some stir," he had to admit, eyeing her monk's habit. Scratching his chin, he suggested, "We could go to my camp, about two miles further."

"For you, it would be better."

"And you?"

"Don't worry about me. Did you ever consider my idea of a standing army?"

"Do you have to be Queen again?" Ariel grumbled as they walked with the horse through a rise between two hills.

"Seriously, it would be a better situation. You would have trained professional soldiers to call on if a war breaks out. Right now, you only have your mercenaries, farmers, tradesmen and riff raff."

"I considered it and I have already talked with the captain of the mercenaries. He thought they would be willing to train recruits. It would mean steady pay and better living conditions. By the way, what happened to my uncle?"

Bortei gave him a sour look, then her anger switched to pity. "I promised him that if he didn't behave, he would be scrubbing pots and pans for the rest of his life. He is at a monastery doing just that."

Ariel looked genuinely shocked. "He is what?"

"You heard me," she said, curtly.

They rode on in silence, sometimes riding and sometimes walking to rest the horse until they came to a rise. Below lay a huge camp.

"Your camp?" Bortei asked.

"Yes. Are you coming with me?"

"No. I'm going home."

"But how?"

"You needn't worry. Anyway, dressed as I am, I would surely be recognized. I bet the story about the Queen and her donkey has already gotten around," Bortei said, her mouth twitching into a smile.

Ariel laughed. "At first, I couldn't believe my eyes. I thought surely that couldn't be you. Lorn was almost beside himself. I think he was embarrassed for you. He never could see the funny side of things."

Bortei gave him an amused look and patted his arm. "I will see you back at the Palace."

"Are you sure you will be all right?"

"I'm sure."

Reluctantly, Ariel rode off, looking back several times.

Bortei waved to him and then walked away. When she was out of sight, she mentally contacted the Silent Ones, and within the next moment, appeared in the living room of her apartment.

"I do love instant travel," she mumbled, nevertheless, ill at ease.

CHAPTER TEN

Later that afternoon, Bortei heard subdued voices coming from her living room. Curious, she went up to the door and noiselessly opened it a slit. There were two strangers who had no business in her private apartment talking in low voices, and a woman was reclining on one of the couches.

The man nearest the couch looked up startled when Bortei suddenly appeared in the room. When he only saw an individual dressed in a monk's habit, his alarm subsided.

Bortei walked up to the couch and looked down at the woman whose eyes were closed. She seemed exhausted. Her clothes looked old and washed out, but had once been of good quality.

Leaning against the wall was a startled Dana. Naturally, she recognized Bortei despite the monk's habit.

"Who is this?" Bortei asked the man nearest the couch.

"This is Isolde Pelias, Lady of Lazar. We are waiting for her son Prince Sinuhe. He went to get a physician."

"Prince Sinuhe's mother," Bortei said, astonished. According to what she knew, Lady Isolde was supposed to be dead. "Where has she been?"

"Lorn Pelias has kept her prisoner in a dungeon. When he was interred in that tower, we freed our Lady and fled with her. We brought her to Azzan for safety. She is exhausted and weak."

Bortei looked at Dana. "Get something hot from the kitchen. If there is any soup, that would be better than tea." she told her.

Dana came back shortly, caring a bowl of soup.

Bortei held the bowl to Lady Isolde's lips. "Here, this is hot, so sip it carefully."

"Thank you," Lady Isolde whispered. With shaking hands, she reached for the bowl.

"I will help you hold it," Bortei told her, and put her own hands around the woman's to keep her from spilling the contents.

When the door opened again, Prince Sinuhe and Tan Rue came in followed by what Bortei surmised to be the physician. Sinuhe stopped in mid-stride when he saw Bortei clad in a monk's habit.

"Lady . . ."

Bortei raised her hand to stop what she was sure was going to be a rebuke. She looked to Tan Rue. "Get Dorcas and see that rooms are readied for Lady Isolde," she ordered quickly.

The physician looked from Prince Sinuhe to Bortei, not sure whom he had before him. The habit meant one thing, but the voice was that of a woman.

"Evans?" Lady Isolde whispered, reaching for her son with her hand.

Sinuhe came to the couch and sat down. He took her hand and said, "It's all right. I will take care of you."

"Sinuhe, she's safe. When she feels better, she can return home. Your father will not trouble her ever again."

"What do you mean?" came his quick rejoinder.

She bent her head slightly to one side and looked at him. "You remember what I promised him if he inconvenienced me again?"

"Yes, I remember."

"He is interred in a monastery."

His eyes opened wide. "Scrubbing pots and pans?" he asked, incredulous.

"Precisely." Bortei rose. "Tan Rue, I could use a bath and then some food."

***

Next morning, she lay in bed going over the previous day and suddenly laughed out loud. "Damned donkey," she muttered, amused.

"Lady Bortei."

Bortei raised her head. Tan Rue looked . . . upset. "Tan Rue, I understand you're put out with me and were worried when you couldn't find me."

He bridled a little. "Lady Bortei, I'm responsible. I'm supposed to take care of you."

"I apologize. But it was important to be where I was and you couldn't come with me. I'm always well guarded. There is no need for you to worry. Now, I'm going through my meditation and exercises. While I'm so occupied, you could find out if Lord Manetho would care to breakfast with me."

His frown disappeared; he was at least partially mollified.

After having finished her morning ablution, Bortei strode briskly toward her breakfast room. When she walked in, Lord Manetho was standing by the window, but turned quickly at the opening of the door. "Good morning, Lady Bortei," he said, bowing slightly.

"Good morning, Lord Manetho. I'm glad you could join me."

After both were seated, Bortei poured his morning drink before Tan Rue, who stood behind her, could do it.

"Now, I bet you have several questions?"

"Lady Bortei, there is a story going . . ."

"And it already came to your ears?"

"Yes, about the Queen in a monk's habit and a donkey," Manetho said, working hard at keeping a somber face.

"Ah, yah, good stories quickly make the rounds. It stopped a stupid, senseless conflict. I would like for Prince Jovan to go to Lazar and use his diplomatic skills there. He especially needs to talk to Prince Sinuhe's older brother. Lorn Pelias is interred in a monastery and will stay there for the rest of his life."

"And Lady Isolde?"

"She can return to Lazar as soon as she feels well enough to travel. Or whatever arrangement Prince Sinuhe sees fit to make for his mother. Now, what happened while I was gone?"

"There is a proposal to appoint a new Finance Minister. The thirty percent tax is on the agenda. Most of the Lords will naturally be against it, and already a few are here to protest, asking for an audience. Will the Queen grant it?"

"No. This falls within Prince Sinuhe's sphere. It will be his job to convince the others that's it is vital and it is the Queen's command."

"Yes, my Lady." He continued briefing her over several other items he thought needed to be brought up for discussion.

After breakfast, both walked in cordial silence to the briefing room. Manetho was beginning to appreciate this Queen and her obdurate single-mindedness. He was intrigued by her and dimly began to perceive the scope of the changes her actions would bring about.

At this briefing, only the consorts were present.

After the meeting, Prince Sinuhe thanked Bortei for the concern she showed for his mother's plight. For the first time, the feeling of rivalry was absent.

Bortei returned to her official office to find a few items on her desk. Most of them were petitions of some sort. Tan T'Sien had carefully weeded out the less important ones. Some she sent back granted; some she wanted more information on, and on some, a note attached to Sinuhe that they were to be denied.

After lunch, she wandered around her apartment, then decided to go for a walk into Azzan. Some time ago, she had told Dana to have simple dresses made so she could go unnoticed through the streets. Before she was finished changing clothes, Tan Rue came into her room and stopped.

"Now, don't you give me that look," she scolded him.

"Lady Bortei, you should not go without an escort."

"And naturally having someone accompany me in a monk's habit would be very incognito."

"Oh, I can change into appropriate attire."

Bortei laughed. "If it will make you feel better, you can come with me."

On their walk through the city, and most of it through the poorest section, Bortei noticed numerous children begging. Most were crippled or had some sort of disfigurement. She and Tan Rue followed a troop going toward a more affluent area of the city.

Intrigued she asked, "Where are those children going?"

He looked at her, his face grim. "Back to their masters," he said, embittered. "Poor parents, often in order to survive, sell their children or abandon them. Many of them are orphaned. They are picked up or bought and then taught to beg or steal. Many are forced to prostitute themselves. It's big business. The ones who keep these children are rich. Many of the children are maimed on purpose to elicit more sympathy."

Aghast, Bortei stared back at him. No, she thought that's nothing new. But her knowledge had only come through literature. She had never thought to encounter it in real life.

"This is heinous."

"It is."

Her face hardened. "Remind me to asked Prince Sinuhe if he ever implemented my proposal to form a professional police force."

"What do you have in mind?"

"To arrest those villains and confiscate their ill-begotten riches."

"They will only bribe themselves out of the charges."

"Not in the courts l will set up. If only it wouldn't take so much time to implement what I'm thinking of. Let's go back home and you will notify the Lord Manetho to ask the Lord Minyar to come to the briefing tomorrow morning."

***

Next morning, she dressed with care. She had designed several Saris, choosing the white one with the gold border.

When she entered the conference room, even the Lord Manetho's eyes lit up in appreciation.

Minyar and Bortei had not seen each other privately since their nuptial nights. They kept their faces bland, only letting their eyes meet for an instant. She greeted the High-Priest with a short bow. "Lord Minyar, my thanks for coming."

Returning the bow, he responded, "Lady Bortei."

"Please be seated." She leafed through the ever-present note book Tan T'Sien carried for her and put it on the table in front of her.

"Prince Sinuhe, a question. Have you initiated forming the police force I suggested?"

"Yes, my Lady. We are in the preliminary phase of setting up a school to educate teachers to teach police procedures. It will take time since this is a new idea."

"Good, keep me informed. Lord Minyar, Prince Sinuhe, there is something of importance I would like to discuss with both of you. I have recently seen the many helpless children who are being exploited and made to work the streets. I want the men or women prosecuted and their riches confiscated. Lord Minyar, I have been told that most of these kids are sold into slavery or are orphans. Can some of your religious orders care for them? Would you have enough manpower to do this? These kids need not only to be housed, but educated. And another thing, they are not to be inundated with religion. I want their aptitude screened. The ones that can be educated, educate them to the limit of their capabilities. The others should learn a trade. I only have a scant idea of the scope of the problem. So your input would be greatly appreciated."

"What my Lady proposes will take time. But I will look into it. There will be a report through Lord Manetho." Minyar rose, and with a short bow left the room.

"Now to other business."

***

Bortei was tired as she pushed the papers to the middle of her desk and rubbed her baldhead. Damn, she thought, I will never get used to not having hair. Wonder if it will ever grow back.

She had been working on several proposals for her tax reform. Her coffers were still empty and the government was running on deficit. At least the governors had agreed to a thirty percent tax if it was for a limited time only. One year should help. She would hate to have riots on her hands. Mostly, the rich protested; the poor were used to being taxed to death. The proposals she had been working on would change that soon. She had closed a lot of loopholes.

As she stretched, the door opened slowly and Jovan came halfway into the room.

"You're still at work?" he asked.

"As you can see. What can I do for you?"

"Mmm, there is a private party. I thought you would like to come."

"What kind of party?"

"A nice one. Our Embassy has invited several foreign dignitaries. You might like to get to know some of them in an informal setting, as Rena."

"I guess I could resurrect Lady Dorcas's niece. What time?"

"In about two hours."

"I'll be ready."

***

They were two streets away from the Embassy when they heard a shout from the driver. The carriage suddenly veered off and turned into another street with the horses at a run.

Jovan rolled the window down and shouted, "What's going on?"

"I lost control. Something else is controlling the horses."

"Can't you stop them?"

"I'm trying, your Highness."

There was a brief familiar mind-touch. Bortei laid her hand on Jovan's arm and said, "I think we are meant to go somewhere else. Tell the driver to relax. It's all right."

The horses pulled the carriage through an open iron gate. Looking up at the house, Bortei thought how it resembled a nightmare out of a horror movie. Hideous gargoyles projected from the gutters and eaves of the building. Inlaid over the lintel was the ugliest mask Bortei had ever seen and two griffins flanked the door.

"Goodness, do you know where we are?"

"Yes, I do. It belongs to the most disreputable individual in all of Atlan.

"And of course you know him."

"Bort . . . Rena, sometimes it's important to know people like that. They have parties and you can pick up a lot of gossip."

"Let's see why we're supposed to come here."

If the house was hideous from the outside, the inside was grotesque. The owner's statement seemed to be 'flaunt all conventions and the more bizarre the decor the better'.

Bortei and Jovan found themselves in the center of a room with frescoed walls and a gilded ceiling. There was a blue, shimmering rug, rose-damasked chairs and love-seats. Overhead was a crystal chandelier reflecting the light from myriads of candles. In a corner was a large group of satyrs and nymphs calculated to bring a blush even to the most decadent cheek.

"Ah, my dear Sasha, we haven't seen you for quite some time." The individual appeared effeminate and his voice was as cool as it was lifeless. His gaze dwelled on Bortei with a remote curiosity. Since Jovan didn't introduce her, he languidly turned away.

"My dear Anper, one needs to take a break from excitement once in a while," Jovan replied in the same languorous voice.

Bortei stared at him as if hypnotized. He seemed to have changed into a completely different personality. The Jovan she knew was full of vitality, but the persona he now exhibited reminded her of a washed up dandy.

"Karson has promised some delightful entertainment for tonight."

"Then I better go and ingratiate myself to him before he considers me an interloper."

They walked away. "What banalities," Bortei whispered to Jovan.

"But dear, flattery can get you a long ways here," he told her, straight-faced.

"Look over there," Jovan pointed to a man who sat as if enthroned in an oversized chair with a ring of devotees surrounding him.

Bortei grunted. What she saw was a restless thin man with a fox-like face.

"Ah, Karson, you are looking well," Jovan greeted him.

There was a sly smile as he looked down at Jovan. Scornfully, he threw up a hand and grunted. He suspected everyone of being false and hypocritical, and he was abnormally suspicious. When he spoke, it was in a rumbling, rusty voice. "Are you returning to us like the prodigal son? We have noted your long absence."

With an exaggerated bow, Jovan said, "I crave your forgiveness if my absence has troubled you."

Karson lifted his hand elegantly and impatiently. "Go enjoy yourself," he said to Jovan, and Bortei was ignored.

"What kind of individual is he?" Bortei asked.

"A very nasty one."

"You know, there are a few faces here I recognize. This here is a similar crowd to the one at the party I went to with Zennor." When Jovan gave her an odd look, she giggled, "Not my kind of parties. So, how come you associate with people like this?"

It's only in the line of duty. There's a lot of useful gossip to be gleaned."

Bortei was amused.

"Can I get you something to drink?" Jovan offered, to divert Bortei's budding curiosity.

"No. I don't think so. I'm still wondering why we are here?"

Jovan shrugged.

During the first part of the evening, Jovan greeted or was greeted by numerous acquaintances. He never introduced Bortei, and she wondered about it.

Later, a door was opened to a room where food was being served buffet style. After all the guests had replenished themselves, they returned to the first room. Suddenly music started up and a dancer came in. He was scantily clad, with a single leaf covering his private area. A groan went up from the audience, mostly men, as he gyrated with the most implicit body language.

"Rena, if you don't want to look conspicuous, wipe that frown off your face."

Eventually, his act was replaced by a troupe of dancing girls who whirled with streamers and shrieked at the top of their voices. In the beginning, the rhythm of the music was almost sedate, but it soon picked up in tempo. The guests became exuberant and the men teasingly tried to fondle the dancers. Shrieking with laughter, they dodged the grabbing hands. Soon the guests joined in the dancing.

Rena, if you don't want to be seen as a party pooper, you better start swaying those hips," Jovan whispered into her ears.

"As long as you stay close by." But that was not possible. Soon they were separated and Bortei was passed from arm to arm.

The party became more boisterous with raucous laughter. Suddenly, the music ceased and only the rhythmic drumbeat continued. At one point, Bortei found herself between two men and both were snatching at her skirt. They tore it off. She was standing there in her bloomers.

Bortei hit one man in the chest and jabbed the other in the back with her elbow. Both men thought it was good sport and tumbled her down to the floor. Kicking and hitting, she gained enough space to get up and run. She escaped from the room and ran down a hallway until she stumbled through another doorway. The next thing she saw was an open door leading out onto a balcony.

Above the balcony was a gargoyle. Bortei clambered up on the rail of the balcony and found a place between the gargoyle's chest and paws. She climbed into it. Taking a deep breath, she leaned back and considered her situation. She couldn't go home in her bloomers, but for a while she was safe.

Not long after, she heard someone stumbling around in the room below and then a curse. Jovan leaning on the doorpost looked up and down the balcony.

"Damned mess. Ouch my knee! Where in the hell did she disappear to?" he groused.

"Sasha," Bortei whispered.

Jovan looked up and laughed. "A hell of a good hiding place," he conceded and climbed up. "Where is the other half of your attire?" he asked, grinning.

"A guy with a black eye and another one with sore ribs tore it off."

"Are you comfortable?"

"Sort of. At least I'm not sliding down."

For a while they leaned back in silence.

"Sasha, I think your hands are roving."

"I'm always fascinated by those slits in the bottom of women's bloomers."

"I bet you are."

"You must concede that the tenor of this party is conducive to arousing this kind of behavior."

"Good excuse." After a considerable time had passed, Bortei asked, "Jovan, don't you think we should join the party again to find out why we are here?"

"If you say so. I like it up here much better."

"Yeah, I bet," and she slapped at his roving hand.

They returned to the other guests. As they entered the room, Anper had just signaled for the music to stop.

"Ah, my dearest friends," he chirped. "I have something special for you tonight."

As he said it, a door opened and four small and naked girls were led in. They were no more than eight or nine years old. Bortei could clearly see how frightened they were. Startled, she looked at Jovan. "What's going on?" she whispered.

Jovan only put his hand on her arm.

Then a golden sculpture was brought in. There was one long stem that branched into four broad leaves. One by one, the little girls were placed on top of the leaves.

Bortei glanced around and noticed that some of the men were getting aroused by the sight. One old man was scratching his crotch. Servants went around the room extinguishing most of the candles, leaving only those illuminating the girls on the sculpture to burn.

"Now, what do we bid for the pleasure of possessing this pristine female flesh?" Anper crooned.

Eager, some of the men surged forward.

"No, no, no!" Anper protested. "No one must touch, only look. Do I have an opening bid?"

The bidding became frenzied while Anper drove the bid higher and higher. It lasted close to an hour. When the last bid was in, the owners wanted to reach for their prizes.

"No, no, no," Bortei's voice was heard. "You mustn't touch," she said, and wagged her finger at them.

Suddenly, four cowled figures appeared beside Bortei holding Karson up between them. A moan went up and several women shrieked, then crumbled unconsciously to the floor.

"Sorry to dismiss you so unceremoniously," Bortei told them, "but the party is over."

Most of the guests couldn't get out of the room fast enough. Only four were somewhat undecided.

"Gentlemen," a voice from the shadow said, "I advise you, it is time to leave."

"But . . . but, our money," one of them spluttered.

"Easy come, easy go," said the pleasant voice.

Bortei craned her neck to see into the dark. She had never heard that voice before and wanted to see who had such a shockingly good sense of humor.

After everyone left, Bortei nodded to the cowled figures and said, "I hope there is enough room at that monastery."

Silently, they disappeared with Karson and Anper. The voice in the dark came forward, a monk from Tan Rue's order.

He bowed. "My Lady, what is your order?"

"Collect the money from the auction. It is for the girls. The rest of the house and its contents are to be auctioned off. The money is also to be used for these little girls."

Suddenly there was a suppressed whimper.

"Oh, my goodness!" Bortei exclaimed. Although only minutes had passed, it must have felt like an eternity to the waiting girls up on the artifact. "I bet you're cold up there," she said, looking up. She reached toward the girl closest to her and said, "Hold on to me and I will get you down."

Bortei lifted all four down and then ordered a servant to bring blankets.

"What are you going to do with them?" Jovan asked.

She looked from him to the girls and scratched the side of her nose. "Yeah, big question."

"We can't leave them here."

The voice in her head said, "Alma, remember when the widow Dorcas talked about Lady Marnie? She is childless and longs for children. Investing the confiscated monies would provide her with an income."

"Good idea," Bortei said, enthusiastically.

"What are you talking about," Jovan asked.

Oops, Bortei thought. "I just had an idea. Dorcas talked to me about Lady Marnie, that she is destitute, and her husband's death left her almost penniless."

Jovan shook his head. "How do you envision these four girls helping?"

"The money Sasha, the money. If well-invested, she could live off the interest. You do have something like that?" she asked, suddenly becoming aware that what she proposed might not be feasible here.

"Yes, we do have investments. I think that with the money here and what the auction will bring, your idea would work. Let's get these poor kids out of here."

Jovan picked up two girls, now wrapped in blankets. And Bortei took the other two and led them out of the house. It was almost morning when they arrived at Lady Marnie's townhouse.

Jovan had the driver pound on the door. Nearly twenty minutes later, the butler came to answer the racket.

"What do you want? It's early and everyone is still asleep."

"We want to see Lady Marnie . . ."

"Haven't you heard? Everyone is still asleep."

"I think the Lady will be glad to be awakened," Jovan told him.

Roused by the noise, Lady Marnie was coming slowly down the stairs. "What's going on?"

"Lady Marnie, it's Sasha. Could I borrow one of your robes for my Lady?"

"Sasha? Oh, it's you. You need a robe?"

"Yes. Please."

She looked at the robe she was wearing, "Sasha, this is the only one I have," she told him, haltingly.

"Oh. My Lady is in something of a state of undress . . ."

"I could lend you one of my wife's," the butler said.

"It would be greatly appreciated. And after you bring the robe, ready a place for four little girls to sleep in."

"Who is your Lady, Sasha?"

"I'd rather not say."

She gave him a penetrating look. "Not one of your . . ."

"No, Marnie, not one of those."

The butler came back and handed Jovan a robe, who went to hand it into the coach.

"The best I can do," he told Bortei.

"Better than walking around in my bloomers."

After Bortei exited the coach, she waved to the others to come closer. Leaning into the carriage, she took out one of the sleeping girls. "Here's one," she said as she handed the girl to Lady Marnie. Again, she reached into the carriage. "Here's two," she told the butler. Then she handed the third girl to Jovan and carried the fourth one into the house herself.

There was a sudden exclamation of surprise from Marnie.

"Is something wrong with the robe?" Bortei asked and lifted her painted on eyebrows.

"No, Lady . . ."

"Lady Marnie," Bortei warned and put her fingers to her lips. "We need a place away from them and then we can talk."

"Ashton, ready the old nursery for the children."

"Yes, Lady Marnie. I'll get my wife up and we'll take care of the children. Come girls, let's go to the kitchen and have some hot milk," he told them.

After the butler left, "Can we go somewhere to talk?" Bortei asked.

"There's a small sitting room upstairs."

"That will be perfect. Let's go there."

The room was small, but cozy and still warm from the heat radiating from the chimney. They had only to wait a short while before the butler announced that the room had been readied and the children were taken care of.

"Tell your wife I'm sorry she was roused out of bed so early. And thank you both," Lady Marnie told him.

"Lady Marnie, those children need someone to care for them and I thought of you . . ."

"But Lady Bortei, I . . ."

"I know. There will be money for you to maintain your establishment and also to care for these children. I don't know where they came from . . ."

"They came from Karson's house," Jovan informed her.

Marnie's hand flew to her mouth and she stifled an exclamation. Stricken, she looked at Bortei and Jovan. "Oh, those poor little ones," she said.

"There will be a monk coming to see you tomorrow and he will set up a financial arrangement. Now, I need to go home; the robe will be returned as soon as possible."

***

It had been a dragging, dreary day. Bortei had sat through a long session with the provincial governors, having to use a lot of persuasion to gain agreements. Each province made its local laws, and because of this, no police force could effectively maintain order. Bortei wanted a national law, also unified laws to raise taxes. Right now, because of the wide spread corruption of public officials, taxes were often extracted by force. Then, these tax monies were squandered illicitly, diverted from public projects. The dissolute aristocracy found it impossible to gather taxes for the national treasury. New departments had to be formed and redundant ones scrapped.

Bortei stood impatiently as each provincial representative bowed before her. By the time the last bowed himself out of the door, she was exhausted. She and Sinuhe were sitting in silence, each busy with their own thoughts.

"Bortei, we need to revise the whole structure of our laws."

"If you want to undertake it, you have my permission. It will be a life project. I studied up on a few of them; many are simply redundant, outdated or ludicrous."

With an ironic twitch of the mouth, he asked, "Will I have to bring them to you for revision?"

Bortei looked at him and shook her head wearily. "I'm simply too tired to spar with you," she told him. "We have an enormous task ahead. Why don't we cooperate?"

Before he could answer, Tan Rue came in to lay out a small table with refreshments. It was a late lunch. The meal consisted simply of fruit and cheese, two small roasted birds, a honey cake and wine. She was lifting a bunch of grapes when her eyes fell on Sinuhe. He was watching her with brooding eyes and she saw his mirthless smile before it disappeared.

She bridled impatiently. "Sinuhe, if you have a grievance, speak of it."

"Her Majesty cares little for me. Why would she cooperate with me?" he said with an effort at controlling the anger he felt.

Annoyed, she asked, "What are you implying?"

"That her Majesty has chosen to ignore me."

"Ignore . . . ?" Bortei stared at him, searching his face. Comprehension finally dawned on what he was implying. Keeping her eyes half averted, she said tartly, "My dear, Sinuhe, I don't plan those encounters, they just happen. Maybe you lack ingenuity, or maybe you don't use your opportunities?"

His expression darkened and then his face became flushed as he glared at her. He rose, "If your Majesty will excuse me," and with a short bow left the room.

Staring at the closed door, exasperated, she mumbled, "Men."

***

Two days later, in the early evening, Bortei entered the library and saw Sinuhe sitting on a couch, several books spread out on a low table.

"What are you reading?" she asked, as she came up from behind.

"I thought about what you said about rewriting these law books . . ."

"And?" she interrupted. Sitting down beside him she looked at what he was reading.

She was sitting so close, her shoulder and thigh touched his. To his chagrin, he became aroused. Bortei was neither beautiful nor possessed the femininity that appealed to him. There were times when he loathed her. But she never bored him; he never found her trivial.

She was straightforward, without artifice. Even in their quarrels, he found satisfaction. She was a worthy opponent.

Blissfully unaware of the havoc she was causing to his hormones, she pointed to the books. "I think we could scrap all these without any damage to the judicial system." When he didn't answer she gave him a quick glance.

With two fingers, he pulled her chin around to kiss her gently on the lips. "How does one invite oneself?"

A flicker of surprise crossed her face and then sudden perception. "Oh," she said, "I will have supper in about an hour. Would you like to join me?"

"I would be delighted."

Chapter Eleven

One sunny, but windy afternoon, Bortei decided to slip out of the Palace. Her neck was stiff and she felt tired. Those sessions are not getting anywhere, she thought. The provincial governors balked at every suggestion she made. Their bullheaded behavior made her consider cutting their power. She wanted cooperation from them, not this constant juggling for a privileged position. It wasn't the first time she thought how childish and stupid they were. As she looked down at Azzan, the only green spot to be seen was where the rich lived. Azzan had no parks.

The slum she had seen was never far from her mind. Today, she thought to investigate it further and donned a slightly tattered servant's dress.

Getting to the slum was farther than she expected. The cobbled streets had ended a long time ago and became a narrow footpath. Again, it was shocking to see so much squalor and poverty. The shanties were built from random material that did not keep the rain or wind out. They were tightly packed with one side being the other's wall. Dust and stench filled the air and her throat tightened. She found it hard to breath. Kids of all ages, most of them naked, began to follow her. The more daring reached out to touch the skirt of her dress. She experienced a slight shiver of fear. She never considered that she could be in any danger. Even in a servant's dress, she was conspicuous here.

As she walked on, she began to itch and wondered if it was just a reaction to the kids scratching themselves. She thought they might have lice, since they were not too clean.

A small troop of soldiers came forward and stopped her.

Their leader, an older man, looked her up and down, then asked, "You're not from here?"

"No, I'm from Legget," Bortei answered him, as she pointed with her thumb behind her. Legget was a little above poor.

"You'd better get out of here. I don't think your lady would appreciate you bringing the plague into her household," he scolded her. "There has already been several outbreaks here. We received orders to cordon this area off."

"Plague? What kind of plague?" she asked alarmed, and felt an urge to scratch herself. "Fleas!" she said, enlightened.

"What do you mean fleas?"

"The cause of the plague are infected fleas," she told him.

He laughed. "That's a new one on me," he told her. "My advice to you is to leave this area."

"How long has this slum been here?"

"You're asking a lot of curious questions, girl. For as long as I can remember. Now, if you are smart, you'll leave here."

"Yes I will, thank you," Bortei told him.

***

When she arrived home, the first thing before even reaching the bathroom was to strip off her clothes and then yell for Tan Rue. After a good scrub down, she asked if the Lord Manetho could attend her.

When he entered her living room, he was not prepared for her immediate question. "How long has the slum down by the market place been in existence?"

Taken by surprise, he replied, "Ever since I can remember. Why?"

"I was told there are already cases of the plague there."

"It breaks out every summer and even spreads to the more affluent houses."

Bortei walked to the window and looked out. It was mid-summer and the two suns, albeit high in the sky, were at aphelion. Only because of this, the land was not burning up.

"Manetho, something has to be done about this slum. I was laughed at when I told someone that infected fleas were causing this plague."

"What do you recommend?" he asked hesitantly, never sure of this Queen's ventures.

"To clean it up. If that ground has been in use for as long as you implied, it has to be saturated with waste. I think it's time . . . to burn it."

"But where will the people go?"

"Don't worry; they're resourceful and will find other places to occupy. Before this summer progresses any further, I want that slum burned down and the other places I have seen cleaned up. Have you ever been down there?"

"No."

"It's an education, Manetho. You need to go and see. The houses are jammed together and the suns hardly shine down into the streets. There are people, even families piled into the doorways. You should smell their bodies and the stale air. You should especially see the children who will never see old age. How would you like to be scared most of your life?"

Manetho winced. "You went there?"

"Yes, on one of my excursions. I even talked to some of the people. They told me of the exorbitant rents being charged. I asked one woman to let me see her place. She took me up to her room. To keep a roof over her head she has sublet it to pay the rent. There were two other families living in there. There is no privacy, no privies, and no water. I found out the landlord only collects the rent and doesn't know who owns the property."

"Most of those places are owned by the gentry. It has made them rich. There are no expenses, so they bring in a lot of revenue."

Bortei turned to look at him. "You must be kidding!"

Manetho hesitated, flustered under her cold stare. "I wish I were."

"Are there any records of who owns those places?"

"Yes, but they are difficult to find."

"You think you could lend me a monk who can full-time investigate?"

"You would risk his life."

"Even if he is sent by me?"

"Yes."

"Heads will roll, Manetho, mark my word. I will not rest until I find the owners. Make sure this is understood."

"Then you are going ahead with your plan?"

"Yes."

"That will cause a lot of consternation."

She looked at his troubled face, "Do you own some of those properties?"

"I'm only a poor monk . . ."

"But does the Temple?"

"I will need to look into that."

"Well, if they do and upgrade those dwellings, I won't say anything."

"I will inquire."

"Also, give notice of the clearing and make sure everyone is out, especially the children and the old."

The fires were set to burn from the outside in, so most of the disease spreading varmints were destroyed. The slum burned for five days before anyone could go in to put out the smoldering embers. There was a near riot, brutally put down by the soldiers.

Bortei did not agree with all that happened.

When spring came, she had trees planted where the slum had been.

***

These tedious sessions. It was not the hours, but getting through recalcitrant minds. Sometimes, she thought, how stupid these men are, and wondered how Sinuhe put up with them. As the routine business of the day continued, Bortei's mind went over various proposals, then listened to the counsel of others and made her decisions. She was the last appeal and her judgment was final.

She sometimes wondered if her efforts were not fated to fail. She envisioned lifting Atlan out of its stagnation. She had visited all eight provinces. She found three with thriving agriculture and prosperous villages. Two were indolent and shiftless and she removed the governors. Two, abutting each other, were thinly populated, the land thickly forested, but with poor and rocky soil. Only Patheon, with Azzan as its capital, had a thriving economy.

Bortei rubbed her eyes. She was tired and abruptly rose.

"None of you have come up with any worthwhile answers. The council will meet again in three months and I adjure you to think about all this and to come up with better solutions." She waited impatiently as each council member bowed themselves out of the chamber. After everyone had left, she went to the window and looked out.

The tediousness of these sessions is never ending, she thought and was startled when the familiar voice in her head said, "Alma, hold onto your hat," and suddenly she was walking down a road toward a village. When she looked down at her clothing, she wore a wide skirt with a blouse and a short, loose jacket.

"Wonder what that beloved Oracle is getting me into this time?" she mumbled.

As she walked toward the village, she could hear the muttering of a crowd. Following the babble of voices, she came to a plaza. It was crowded. Bortei's eyes were immediately drawn to a gallows with a ready noose.

"What's going on?" she asked a man who stood next to her.

"They're going to hang him and he didn't do it. We all know he didn't do it. He was framed."

"What was he supposed to have done?"

"Murdered a monk and taken his purse."

"Was there much money in the monk's purse?"

"Are you kidding? They come around and beg for alms."

"Did the Monk have money on him?"

"No, but they found his purse at Oral's house and arrested him. It was full of coins."

"How did Oral get the purse?"

"He doesn't remember. He was drunk."

"Why would anyone frame him?"

"We suspect because he owns that rich bottom land down by the river. It's happened before." The man pointed to a castle on top of a hill. "He's the one who wants to own all the land around here. If you don't sell, he finds some other way to get it; like framing poor old Oral."

Bortei, standing next to her informant, wondered if she should intervene herself, or have her newly appointed judicial investigator brought here. She went down into meditative levels and sent out a questioning thought.

"Go to the lone oak tree and meet him there," she was told.

Oak tree, she thought, and meet whom? Leaving the crowd, she looked around. Oh! That oak tree. It was a giant tree in full splendor standing by itself in the center of a meadow.

As she walked toward the tree she could see Uslio, her newly appointed troubleshooter. He was leaning against the tree's bole looking totally confused.

"Uslio," she called softly. He looked at her but didn't recognize who she was. "Uslio," she said again and walked up to him. "I'm sorry. I know it's shocking, but I need you. Come, walk beside me and I will fill you in."

Finally, he recognized the voice, if not the person standing before him. "My Lady . . ."

"Don't Uslio, just listen," and she told him the story she had been told.

When she was finished, he asked, "What do you want me to do?"

"Investigate."

"I don't think I can command much authority by myself." As he said it, a troop of eight soldiers appeared riding through the meadow toward the village.

"There is your backup," she told him, and handed him her signet ring. "Go talk to them."

When Uslio approached the troops, the commanding officer alighted from his horse and instantly recognized Uslio.

"Hey, Uslio, what are you doing here?" They were old childhood friends and had grown up on the same street.

"Boy, Marcher, are you a Godsend. I need you to back me up." Then he told Marcher why he was there, but not *how* he got there. He didn't mention that the Queen was also present.

Marcher turned back to his troops, "Look sharp, we need to impress those folks and make sure my friend here doesn't get short changed. And get him a horse so he can ride into this village. It will look more dignified than walking."

Marcher and Uslio mounted the horses and rode into the village. The magistrate and his court were just coming out of the courthouse. Two policemen were leading a shackled man between them.

Bortei watched from among the crowd as the Judge walked up to a podium and the prisoner was led to stand in front to face the crowd.

A clerk had begun to read the verdict when Uslio with Marcher and his troops rode in.

Uslio rode up to the clerk and took the sheaf of paper from his hand. "I think this needs a little more looking into," he told the Judge.

The Judge's gavel came down and he shouted, "How dare you interrupt these court proceedings."

"I am Uslio Sura, newly appointed legal envoy of her Majesty, Queen Bortei."

"I don't care who . . . what did you say?"

"I'm the legal envoy of her Majesty, Queen Bortei." He then held up the signet ring for all to see. "And who are you?"

"I am Keel, the District Judge."

"I'd like to see . . ."

The noise of galloping hooves interrupted Uslio, and the crowd swiftly parted to make room for a rider who stopped in front of the podium. Spinning his horse in a circle, he saw the soldiers and reigned in his horse. His eyes narrowed until they were glittering slits as he looked at Marcher.

"What's the meaning of this?" he bellowed.

"I'm Captain Marcher, attaché to Uslio Sura, judicial envoy of her Majesty, Queen of Atlan. And you?"

He looked at him warily. "I am Exuviae, Baron of Gnawer," he said crisply.

"My Lord, you are disrupting the judicial proceedings here," Captain Marcher told him, keeping his voice low.

"I will let you know if I disrupt or not. Judge Keel, continue with the proceedings."

"My Lord, I can't. Lord Uslio is the Queen's appointed Judge and he has ordered an investigation into this court's proceedings."

"Says who?" he thundered.

"The Queen of Atlan. If you don't comply, I will have you arrested, in the name of the Queen." Uslio told him.

Before Bortei left, the prisoner was returned to his cell and Uslio had asked to see all the evidence.

***

It was such a nice day and Bortei was loath to going back to the Palace. She walked along a tree-lined country road and considered going on to the next village. Walking had given her an appetite, so she decided to have a break and get something to eat in one of the country inns.

Before entering the village, something nudged her mind, telling her to walk along the outskirts of the town. There was a small temple standing on top of a knoll and as she came closer she could hear children's voices reciting.

Attached to the temple were several small buildings and on a lawn, a group of children were listening to a lecture under a shade tree. The lecturer was a spindly and austere looking monk.

As Bortei drew closer, she could make out the words. The lecture was more of a harangue and as she listened she became more and more outraged. Quietly, she inched closer and then suddenly loomed up in front of the Friar. "What are you preaching, my dear Brother?" she asked sweetly.

"I'm instilling righteousness and the fear of God in these children," he told her with fiery eyes.

Hmm, she thought, we have a zealot here preaching his personal creed. "But why would the children need to fear God?"

"To obey his commandments and to lead a righteous life."

"But my dear Brother, usually we hate what we fear. Do you want God to be hated?"

"You are a woman and don't understand these things. God is supreme above all else. Humanity needs to worship him. He is omniscient and omnipresent in all things," the monk intoned, his voice rising with a mellifluous resonance.

"Ah, yes, but if God is above humanity, why does he need to be worshipped? Don't you think that is a human need . . . ?" the monk tried to cut her off but she raised her hand. "Don't tell me again that I'm a woman and don't understand these things. I understand that fear engenders hate, but love, compels respect. I'd rather be loved and respected than feared and hated."

The children had listened with rapt attention. It wasn't so much what Bortei said, but that she had called down the not-so-very-loved Brother. But she quickly lost their attention when two Brothers, one carrying a huge pot and the other dishes, walked toward a picnic table.

"It's time for a repast," said the one with the pot as he put it on the table. He was rotund with a cheerful and benign expression. The children immediately moved to gather around him.

"Brother Read, I have not finished with my instruction," the lecturing Brother complained.

Brother Lace, one can't listen with an empty stomach."

"You are overindulging these children."

"A little indulgence goes a long way," Brother Read told him, unperturbed.

Bortei listened, amused at their exchange and was about to leave when Brother Read stopped her with, "Lady, it's not much, but would you care to share our meal with us."

"Smells good," she told him and promptly took a seat on the bench. It was some kind of stew made with the vegetables they grew and it was delicious.

"You seem to like children," Bortei said to Brother Read.

"Who wouldn't?" he told her. "I like their exuberance and sheer joy in living."

"Then why does Brother Lace teach them all about gloom and doom?"

"Brother Lace envisions himself as a reformer."

"So his sentiment is not shared by everyone?"

"At least not by me," Brother Read said and chuckled.

"Who is your superior?"

"That would be Abbot Anselm, and he is just coming over to join us."

Bortei studied the approaching man. Father Anselm was a big man, long-boned and wide-shouldered. He had a long face and deep-set eyes.

"Please remain seated," he said as he approached. "I see we have a lady to share our repast. I'm sorry we can't offer you better."

"No apologies needed. This stew is delicious," Bortei told him.

"What brings you to our temple?"

"A chance to talk to you."

"I'm interested."

"It can wait until you have eaten."

After the tables were cleared and the children had left, he looked at her with a smile. "Now, what have you to talk to me about?"

"The children, they are orphans?"

"Yes. My abbacy covers three counties. We try to gather the orphans before someone else gets a hand on them. The world is wicked. Do you believe in evil?"

"In evil, yes. I have seen enough of it."

"You are not of our faith?"

"If it is what I heard Brother Lace instructing the children in, I am not."

"He gets carried away sometimes."

"That is no excuse. Father Anselm, he is to be kept away from the children." Her words came out as an order.

Father Anselm looked searchingly at her face. "Lady, I think you are not what you appear to be."

"That's neither here nor there. Of your order, are there others who gather children?"

"I have been asked by the High-Priest, the Lord Minyar, to sound out other members of my order to see if they would be willing to open orphanages."

"I see. Keeping it small and local, that would be a better idea," Bortei said musingly, but more to herself. "Yes, I think that would be better. But Father Anslem, see to it that they select individuals like Brother Read. He loves and enjoys children. Being orphaned is bad enough, without having a Brother Lace thrown in," she said and beamed at him.

"I see what you mean. There is going to be a meeting with several of my brother Abbots. I will convey your wishes. Lady, with your permission?" he rose and bowed.

Bortei watched him leave. *I think we will meet again.* She was sure of it. Still not willing to go back home, she sighed. It was just too nice. It was like a spring day, a breeze gently rustling the leaves and the sun shining from a deep blue sky.

Reluctant to leave the peaceful place, she heaved herself off the bench. She retraced her steps until she was again on the tree-lined country road. Since she had eaten, she thought to skirt the village. The road was beginning to go steeply up a hill and when she came around a bend, she saw a man whipping a horse hitched to an overloaded wagon.

"Hey, knock it off," she hollered at him. "Don't you see she can't handle the load?"

Infuriated, he yelled, "If I wanted your stupid advice, I'd ask," and began hitting the horse again.

Enraged, Bortei snatched the whip away and began applying it to him. "You dumb, stupid idiot. Can't you see she's giving you all she can?"

The old man shrieked in frustrated anger as he tried to cover at least his head from the impact of the whip.

Panting for breath, Bortei finally stopped. "You stupid, old man," was all she could say as she looked down on him. A snort from the horse made her aware of the animal again. "Ah, and you're dumb, too. I would have kicked the shit out of him if I were you."

She went over to the horse and unhitched her.

"What are you doing?" the old man hollered.

"What am I doing? I'm going to let you pull your wagon all by yourself," she told him and walked away.

"You can't do this to me!"

"Well, I've done it."

"Help me to at least catch my horse."

Without looking back, Bortei began trudging up the hill. In her anger, she had exhausted herself. The last thing she heard was the old man yelling, "Bring my horse back!"

She stopped, wondering what the hell he was talking about. Suddenly, she received a gentle nudge on her back to go on. The horse, a medium tall mare with every rib showing and sway backed like a hammock had followed her.

Turning around, Bortei told her, "Hey this was not in the bargain." But the mare just stood there hanging her head and snorted.

"You're a mangy looking thing. Everyone will laugh and think it an insult if I bring you to the Palace stables. Even the horses will snicker at you."

But the mare was not deterred by anything Bortei told her and fell in right behind her.

When she came to a pasture at the edge of a forest, she went to lie beneath a tree. It had gotten a little warmer than was comfortable, and she thought to rest for a while. That was all right with the horse. She had found a puddle left over from the last rain and then began to graze.

Bortei, lying under the tree, began to look at the sky. I wonder what that is, she thought. It was not one of the moons she knew. But there was a point of light in the sky. Since there were no airplanes, it couldn't be landing lights. Then it didn't seem to move. She was intrigued by it and decided to ask Manetho.

She must have fallen asleep, because she was awakened by a fly buzzing around her nose. She slapped at it and became more fully awake. The horse was still there, drowsing sleepily.

Bortei began walking away and was nearly back to the country road when the mare was again behind her. "You're the proverbial bad penny," she mumbled. She turned around and stoking her muzzle, she asked, "You mind being called Penny?"

She received a snort into her ear and a gentle nudge. "Yes, I know it's time to go home. I have been truant long enough."

After an hour, she came to the outskirts of Azzan and in another half hour she entered the paddocks for the Palace horses.

Nobody was in sight, so she went to the stables. She walked down the center aisle; it had stalls on both sides. The stalls which housed the Prince's horses were marked with the Royal insignia. After a moment, Bortei became aware that Penny was no longer following her. When she turned around, she saw that Penny was hobnobbing with the other horses. She had gone up to a stall and nickered softly and the horse was nuzzling with her.

"What's going on?" One of the grooms had come out of the tack-room.

"I need to find a place for my horse," Bortei told him, as she pointed at Penny.

When he saw Penny, he began to laugh. "What do you want with that old nag? The other horses will be embarrassed to have her here."

"If you will observe, they're nuzzling each other. People are snobs; horse are much more equitable."

The groom walked up to Penny and looked her over, noticing the stripes left by the whip. "This horse had been abused," he said, outrage in his voice.

"I know. But now the former owner sports some stripes himself."

There was a short, "Oh! Good for you." His attitude softened as he said, "I think I can find a place for her. There's a paddock that's empty right now. We can put her in there."

"Thank you. What's your name?"

"Dabir."

"Dabir, if you could get her to follow you instead of me, I'd be very grateful," Bortei said with a winsome smile.

"Let's put her in that paddock. If she's happy there, she'll stay."

"You know a lot about horses?"

"I started out as a stable boy. Now I'm foreman." When he reached for Penny's halter, she reared up.

"She's still frightened, but she will follow me," Bortei told him.

"I'll get a small bucket with oats," he told her.

"I'm not sure if she knows what oats are."

"Don't worry, she'll learn quickly."

As they left the stables, sure enough Penny came trotting along. When Dabir opened the gates to the paddock, Penny only stood studying the situation. But as soon as Bortei stepped through, Penny followed. Bortei walked up to a windbreak. There was a hayrack and a bucket mounted on the wall for the oats.

"Dabir, give me the oats and let's see what she does with them." Bortei emptied the container into the bucket on the wall and Penny, being curious, pushed her away. She put her nose into the bucket and sniffed the oats then started to nibble at them with her lips. One taste was all it took and she began eating. "I told you she'd learn quickly." But when Bortei tried to leave, Penny came after her.

"You have something of yours to leave with her?"

Bortei patted at her blouse and then her skirt. "I have a handkerchief."

"That might do it."

Bortei took it out and going back into the shack, tied it to the hayrack. Penny sniffed the handkerchief then put her nose into the hay. Bortei patted her rump and left. Penny only turned her head to look over her shoulder. "I'll be back," Bortei promised.

CHAPTER TWELVE

It was darn hot and mid-summer. Bortei, out for a walk with Penny, studied the two suns. Both were now high in the sky and burning down. It would be another three hours before the first sun would touch the horizon.

Bortei trudged up the steep hill with Penny faithfully following behind. The horse responded well to a halter with reins and a light saddle Bortei had chosen so she would not be too burdened. Penny had recovered nicely since being freed from her cruel owner. Now she plodded beside Bortei with her nostrils extended. She probably smelled the cool air under the pines, and Bortei suspected there was likely water ahead. The air did feel at lot cooler when she entered the forest. Suddenly Penny tried to forge ahead. Aha, water Bortei thought and released the reins, then followed at a slower pace. When she caught up with Penny, she stood beside a tarn, drinking. It was a small mountain lake surrounded by a thick stand of pines. Bortei looked around. It was quiet, no other sound except birds and forest noises. Bortei removed the saddle from Penny and opened the saddlebags to take out a second change of clothes.

"You don't mind me wearing my birthday suit?" she asked Penny, who only snorted lightly and nuzzled Bortei's ear.

"I thought you would agree."

Bortei's clothing consisted of light cotton slacks and a v-neck blouse. After stripping, she cautiously approached the water. It was cold in spite of the hot day. Slowly, she eased herself in. Soon she was completely wet; the water felt marvelous and tingly. After about twenty minutes, she emerged from the water only to realize she had no towel to dry off. Suddenly, a hand holding a towel reached over her shoulder. She gave a startled gasp and quickly grabbed the towel and wrapped herself in it before turning around. She had expected Tan Rue, but this was a total stranger, a monk.

"I hope you feel refreshed now," he said, almost as if he were in the habit of handing towels to naked ladies.

"How long have you been here?" Bortei asked, slightly embarrassed.

"I saw your horse come through the trees."

"Oh, that long."

"My name is Tan Sung. Somehow, I was guided to come here and I thought to meditate. But I have a feeling that was not what I was meant to do. Can I try out an idea I have?"

"You might. But first I need to dress. Then I have some bread and apples if you don't mind sharing them with me?"

Bortei dressed, then sat down with a tree log as a backrest and handed a slice of bread and an apple to Tan Sung.

"To make things easier, you can call me Rena," and pointing to the contently grazing horse, added, "That is Penny."

"I belong to a contemplative order. But I have always felt that praying and chanting was not enough, at least not for me. I need to do something. I like to use my hands. I thought maybe I could start an order taking care of the sick and dying, something more useful," he said earnestly.

Bortei eyed him speculatively. She was not so much concerned with the sick and dying, but with the plight of the children she had seen. They had looked starved and abused. She had even seen two and three year olds begging in the streets or rummaging through garbage for something to eat. She sat for some time contemplating Tan Sung.

"Did you discuss this with your Superior?"

He lifted both shoulders up to his ears and released a big sigh. "Yes, I have. But his response was that since ours is a contemplative order, that's what I should be doing and not spinning fancy daydreams. Do you think I'm that much out of line?"

"No. I can understand your compassion for the sick. How would you start with founding an Order?"

"There are brothers who are in agreement with me, but are too timid to voice their desires, knowing the Prior's objections." Tan Sung smiled at her; his smile had an extraordinary charm.

"Have you ever considered the plight of the children?"

"Yes, many times. I've thought about them on many sleepless nights. But I don't know how to begin. There are so many, and I don't have any idea what to do with them."

"Have you ever thought about educating them?"

"That would be a humongous task."

"Yes, I understand. To treat the sick, you would have to have physicians. To educate children, you would have to have teachers. And to deal with children you would have to teach about children and how to recognize their needs. You're correct in that it would be a Herculean task."

Tan Sung regarded her for the longest time, then sank into a prolonged period of silence. "You have not only shared your bread and apples with me, but given me food for thought," he told her.

"Go into Azzan and see the High-Priest and tell him that on your travels you met a woman name Rena. Then tell him your story."

"And will he listen to me?"

"Yes, if you mention the name Rena."

"Who are you?"

"I'm a sojourner and I travel these lands with my ear to the ground, listening to the heartbeat of this world." She gave him a mischievous smile and began gathering her belongings.

***

Bortei had just entered the conference room and was surprised to see the Lord Minyar by the window in an earnest discussion with Prince Sinuhe.

All conversation stopped and everyone turned to face her.

"Good morning, Lady Bortei."

"Good morning, Lord Minyar. Good morning gentlemen and please be seated."

When everyone was seated, she asked, "Business of the day?"

Minyar gave a quiet cough.

"Yes?" Bortei asked.

"There was a monk named Tan Sung asking for an audience. He mentioned the name Rena."

"I see. And what did you say to his idea?"

"We discussed it. What you have in mind would work for Azzan and the other cities, as well as the countryside. If we make it a local concern, this idea could be workable. He conceded it would take time to train people to know how to properly take care of children.

"It is important to make a beginning."

CHAPTER THIRTEEN

Arion had been sent by the Hidden Ones to question Master Ashir and Lord Manetho about the Queen's progress. Now he was on his way back out of their mountain dwelling after telling them what he'd found. They were not too pleased. His report showed no new developments.

As he walked back toward his apartment, he entered an unknown corridor by mistake. It led deep inside the hollowed out mountain. He came upon a stone formation, which at first he thought was natural, then realized they were sculptures rising from the cave's floor. Enchanted, he walked from one to the other, running his eyes and his hands in appreciation along the folds and curvature. Suddenly he came upon a prism reflecting a light from above into a rainbow. His ascetic contemplation was interrupted by twittering voices. They seemed to be coming from a crater in the floor. Curious, he silently moved closer. By stretching out on the floor, he was able to edge near the rim.

Below, in a huge cavity, there were what looked like tiny children with multi-colored wings. How beautiful, he thought. But there was something that disturbed him. The fairy-like children should be at least happy, or laughing, even. Instead, they were huddled in a corner, seemingly, frightened. A bright light suddenly streamed in from a slowly opening door, and they began twittering in agitation. Soon he saw what was causing their panic. A creature, something that reminded him of a fat gray worm encased in numerous folds of rough skin entered the room, waving four arms and hands and walking on two legs. The fairies' agitation grew. And suddenly Arion knew why. Terror. He had never experienced it himself; he had never known any degree of fear or terror. The worm's head was thick and round, without a neck. It had been moving from side the side and suddenly his tongue had flicked out. There was a scream as it caught one of the fairies. To Arion's shock and revulsion, the worm devoured the child-like pixie.

Arion pressed both hands to his mouth to stop the rising shriek. Cautiously, he slithered backward and then in his heedless flight, stopped only when he had reached the long corridor. Panting, he slowly sank to the floor with his arms wound around his head. What he had seen horrified him and cast the Hidden Ones in an entirely new light.

From then on, he began watching them by using the long corridor he had happened upon, his means to penetrate their domain. One day, he came upon a group of the Hidden Ones lying on long couches. "What reason did Manetho give for the Queen to reject this new invention?" Arion heard someone say.

"He said that she thought it would pollute the air."

"But she did accept the idea about the oil?"

"Yes, but only for restricted usage."

"She is growing difficult."

"I wonder how long it will take for these Atlantes to be able to repair and keep up with our technology."

"Maybe in another twenty years. By then, the Queen's clone will have grown enough to take her place."

Slowly Arion backed away and cautiously made his way to his apartment. Until now, his forays into their territory had remained undetected. In order to keep his absences secret, he arranged his bed to look like he was sleeping in it. So far the ruse had worked.

From then on, he analyzed the questions asked of Master Ashir more thoroughly, searching for the meaning behind them. What emerged from his efforts was that the Hidden Ones were waiting for Atlan to be raised to a level of civilization and technology in which they would be able to exist. They obviously looked on humans only as potential slaves.

***

One day, an emissary from the Hidden Ones asked Arion to investigate Master Ashir. They deemed the Queen's progress too slow and were becoming impatient.

Arion knew all about Master Ashir. He knew that he had no parentage and had been created by the Hidden Ones. Arion was physical perfection, while Ashir, albeit younger, had always looked like an old man.

When Ashir entered the cathedral size room, Arion rose from a throne-like chair and asked if he would like to walk while he conveyed the orders of the Hidden Ones.

Ashir showed his surprise by raising his eyebrows. "Yes, since I have been sitting in my office for the better part of the day and the weather is pleasant, a walk would be salutary."

As they tried to leave by the door Ashir had entered, Arion was met by a force field he couldn't penetrate. It took him only a second to realize that he was a prisoner, that he had always been a prisoner. It had never entered his mind before to leave his domicile. It had been perfect and tailored to his desires.

"To understand, I need to see," Arion said to the room.

"No one is to see you," came a disembodied voice from the back of the room.

"I will wear a robe."

After a short wait the force field came down. Outside the door a man handed him a robe. After he donned it, Ashir and Arion walked with unhurried strides down the corridor and then up a long flight of stairs to the mouth of a cave. In front of them was a boulder-strewn basin.

Astonished, Arion looked at Ashir. "Does the outside all look like this?" he asked.

"No. Come follow me."

Ashir led him along a narrow path to a small ridge and over to a meadow speckled with wild flowers.

"Somewhat better," Arion said with a twitch to his mouth.

"Come, there's a small copse and we can sit in peace."

They walked toward a stand of firs and Ashir, tucking his habit under his knees, sat on the ground.

"Now, what is it you want to convey to me and for you to see?" Ashir asked him after he was seated.

"The Hidden Ones are getting impatient with the Queen's slow progress. To understand it, it is essential that I see."

"Then we need to go to the Temple."

Ashir activated a device on his wrist and in seconds both appeared at the Temple in Ashir's office.

"Fascinating," Arion said. "Does everyone travel this way?"

"No. Travel is by foot or on horses," and with a tight smile, Ashir told him, "This is a gift from the Hidden Ones." Ashir rang a hand bell and shortly, a monk opened the office door.

"Master Ashir?" he asked.

"Tan Nun, please have a carriage at the north door."

After the monk closed the door quietly behind him, Ashir said, "I think a ride through the city and the country side should be enlightening. Now, let's walk through the cloister."

The place had a well-worn appearance which bespoke of its age and long use. The stone walls appeared ancient and were deep within the bowels of the earth. Monks walked along the corridors individually or in pairs. Doors opened and closed automatically. The place was a busy hive. Suddenly they came upon a Monk mopping the floor and Arion stopped to observe. He had never seen this before. Ashir, touching his arm, reminded him to walk on.

When they came out at the north door, Arion stopped and stared, seeing another sight that was new to him. He knew about horses, but had never seen live ones. The carriage was large and by present standards luxurious with an upholstered interior and large windows on the doors to look out.

"What is this?"

"Our transportation," Ashir told him. "Come, enter."

As the horses started to pull away from the curb, Arion's eyes opened in alarm and he grabbed the seat with both hands.

"There is nothing to worry about," Ashir assured him. "Observe through the window on your door."

Ashir leaned back in his seat and watched Arion as they rode through Azzan. Throughout their ride, Ashir came to the conclusion that everything they encountered was an unusual experience for Arion.

After a while, Ashir stopped the carriage and told the driver to get some refreshments for them.

"You have never seen any of this?" Ashir asked.

"No. I have always been in what I considered my world. I did not know there was anything outside of it."

"Where did you think I came from?"

"They said from the Temple. But I had no idea what or where the Temple was. I was only to report what you told me. It was not necessary for me to understand."

Ashir shifted his position and wondered what kind of questions he might ask. He was taken aback when Arion asked, "Do you know who or what the Hidden Ones are?"

"No. I know they only speak through intermediaries, and the only one I've ever met is you."

Arion had thought long and hard on how to approach this and was pondering what opening to use when Ashir discerning his thoughts said, "You can trust me. This is why we came here in the carriage. No one can overhear us here."

Arion took a deep breath. "Have you ever wondered at the aim of the Hidden Ones?"

"It is not benevolent?"

"Are you guessing, or did you come to the conclusion yourself?"

"Arion, we need not tiptoe warily around each other. I told you, you can trust me. I am trusting you just by being here. I have wondered for a time about where the orders and questions were leading."

"Master Ashir, they are not human."

It had never occurred to him that they could be something else. "How do you know?" he asked sharply.

"Because I've seen them." Arion then related how he had taken the wrong turn and what he had observed.

Ashir looked profoundly shocked. "But they seem to be intelligent."

"Yes, I suspect to a high degree. Also, they appreciate beauty. All their creations are ascetically pleasing, but there seems to be a callousness toward other life forms not their own."

"That is apparent."

"What do you advise me to do?"

"For the time being, we will continue as we have. The Queen is making great strides." With a ghost of a smile, he continued, "She's cleaning up the mess she says she was dropped into. We will bide our time. You observe, but do not put yourself in peril. As you said, they are intelligent, so be watchful. We will report as we always have, but will take more care of our wording."

"And the Queen?"

"I will see that she is protected."

The driver came back with the refreshments he had been asked to purchase. They ate as the carriage rolled through the city and later through the countryside as Ashir explained the different layers of society.

***

When Arion entered his world again, it seemed wanting. It was still ascetically pleasing without ugliness, but empty of the exhilaration that life brought. He sat in his chair contemplating his new dilemma when the voice from the wall said, "Now, what have you found out?"

"That everything is progressing satisfactorily in accordance with the people's mentality which, as I perceived, is not very highly developed."

"But is there progress made?"

"Yes. Slowly, but surely. Master Ashir reports that the Queen is instituting learning centers. It will take a generation or so before any progress will be apparent."

"Then, Master Ashir is satisfied with the progress made?"

"Yes, very."

***

Master Ashir and Lord Manetho were having what looked like an amiable conversation as they strolled through the Palace grounds. Some time ago, even before this revelation, it had dawned on Master Ashir that Arion was also created and was not one of the Hidden Ones. He was beautiful, a perfect creation. But since mind was added, so was the possibility of rebellion. As they walked, Ashir conveyed this to Manetho and the information that Arion had given him.

"Will he help the Queen?" Manetho asked.

"Yes. Astonishing, isn't it. He said that the Hidden Ones are not human. I don't know if his sense of beauty was outraged or the use he was put to."

"And he has promised to relate to us any information he can gather about the Hidden Ones?"

"I think he has a highly developed sense of equity. It was the first time he had seen any other life forms, such as animals. He was amazed at the variety and also amused by them."

"His world must seem a bit devoid after that."

"I can imagine. From what we know so far, there is very little we can do. Now the question is, do we inform the Queen? You know her better than I do."

"Master Ashir, we can only stand back and watch. It would serve no purpose to alarm her. It is still early in the game."

CHAPTER FOURTEEN

Bortei's rule over Atlan has lasted five decades. During that time she has tried her best to push back the tide of decay and dissipation. The Nobles have obeyed her, but do not love her. She has no room for sentimentalities. Since the beginning of her reign, her objective has been to maintain a balance between the provinces through cooperation so no one province could become strong enough to overwhelm another.

The relationship between Bortei and Prince Sinuhe has become an amiable one, especially after he realized she was gladly leaving the governing of Atlan to him. He had been prepared and trained for it. The love between her and Lord Minyar has deepened and is now an abiding friendship.

One unexpected boon developed. Tan Rue and Dana had children who are now Bortei's domestic attendants. When she asked Tan Rue how they managed this, he glibly replied, "the natural way." Albeit, being a monk, he had not been required to take the vow of celibacy. Now that he is old, he is being cared for by his children and is able to watch them take care of the Queen.

Gradually, the orphans, because of their education, have become a changing influence in society. They are part of a new class within the societal structure, a class of Artisans. There is still poverty, but the gap between the rich and the poor is not as stark. Already, there are citizens who desire a better life for their children through the improved education system.

Manetho, because of age, retired. Bortei's new adviser, the Lord Istavan, seems less flexible, more uncompromising, if not hostile.

Before Master Ashir withdrew, he imparted to her the aim of the Hidden Ones, their calculated waiting for Atlan's civilization to reach a certain level, then dispense with Bortei and take over. Their reign would be total tyranny.

Bortei had pondered over this for a very long time. Then one morning she went into her meditation room, calling on the Oracle.

"Alma, you're troubled," the voice said to her mind.

"Yes. What are we to do about these Hidden Ones?"

"Because of you, and because of a meeting you will have, they will not succeed."

"Am I to worry about them?"

"No. Only be watchful."

"Who are they, if I am allowed to know this now?"

"Aliens who came to this world. At first, they were few in number. Now they have increased considerably. They have tried several times to take control, but were foiled. The last Queen became aware of them too late and destroyed what technology there was. She instigated the wars between the different factions."

"Did they remove her?"

"No. They are not in control of the Oracle."

"Well, that's one good thing," Bortei quipped.

There was a gentle chuckle and the Oracle was gone.

***

One morning, as she entered her living room, Matyas, Tan Rue's eldest son, was waiting for her. "Lady Bortei, Prince Sinuhe is calling for you. His illness has worsened and I have summoned the physician."

"Thank you, Matyas. I will go to him now." She entered his bedroom and momentarily closed her eyes. "How is he?" she asked the physician.

"He is conscious now."

When Bortei stepped up to the bed, Prince Sinuhe turned his head to smile at her. He had aged while she had grown younger as had Minyar. Years ago, Manetho had told her this would happen. When she asked if it was the reason she had lost her hair, he confirmed it.

Prince Sinuhe's voice was quite weak when he spoke. "Come, sit. You have been worried about something?"

Taking his hand, she sat down on his bed. "What makes you think I'm worried about something?"

"Bortei!"

"It's nothing that needs our immediate attention. Now, how are you feeling?"

"Lousy. This pain in my chest, it won't go away; it's making me feel weak. You haven't come to brief me for several days."

"There was nothing of importance."

"But I still like for you to come."

"I was here, but you were asleep."

Suddenly a convulsion wracked his body. When the physician tried to move Bortei aside, Sinuhe held onto her.

"Where is Matyas?" Bortei asked.

"He has gone to get the Lord Minyar."

"Good. Please, let the physician look at you," Bortei begged him.

"Love . . . not long."

169

"Sinuhe, please!"

"Bortei?" Minyar had come up beside the bed and she moved to make room for him. He brushed his hand across Sinuhe's brow. Bortei gave him a troubled look. Sinuhe was the last of her consorts. Jovan had been killed in a meaningless duel and Ariel was fatally crushed when his horse fell on him.

"Evans, let your physician look at you, please," Minyar insisted, using his old name.

With his eyes fixed on Bortei, he asked Minyar, "You will take care of her?"

"Yes. I will take care of her," he promised.

"There's something going on. There's a danger. I don't know. I've sensed it for a long time."

"Evans, she will be all right."

"I don't like Istavan." Turning to Bortei, "Beware of him," he said, agitated and reached for her hand.

"I'm aware of him," Bortei assured him, holding his hand between hers. "I have been watching him."

"Good . . . Zennor . . . take . . ." were Sinuhe's last words as a shudder racked his whole body. His eyes closed and his last breath left his body in a long sigh.

Bortei sank down on his bed, her head resting on his chest. After a while, Minyar took her shoulders to raise her up. "Bortei come, let the physician do his thing."

He led Bortei back to her living room. They sat down on the couch with Bortei clutching him.

Chapter Fifteen

Bortei had achieved many improvements for Atlan and she had expanded the country by diplomacy rather than military conquest. Several smaller countries, for protection from their larger neighbors, and also for commerce, had formed an alliance with her. Bortei had granted them self-government and only insisted that they adopt Atlans laws. The laws had been Sinuhe's life work. He had revamped the legal system, totally changing the old laws. He had also set up a more equitable wage system and an efficient system for taxation. She had relinquished most of the governing to him. Only the provincial governors still reported directly to her and she insisted on a detailed briefing. After Sinuhe's death, she was urged by her provincial governors to select a successor. Many hoped that her choice would fall to one of them.

"When I'm ready to select a new Governor, I will inform you, and the choice will be mine," Bortei told them coldly. "Now, if you gentlemen will excuse us, I have things to discuss with the Lord Minyar."

Having been so peremptorily dismissed, all they could do was bow themselves out the door.

"You're walking a thin line," Minyar told her.

"I know. But if I let them get away with it, I would soon lose control. Do you know what they're after?"

"They don't know what they are doing or why, but they are following a course which will give the Hidden Ones control over Atlan."

"Like Arion said, the Hidden Ones want to enslave the people of Atlan to serve their end, and I'm in their way. Atlan has progressed far enough toward the technology they find livable," Bortei said.

"When did you first become aware of the Hidden Ones?"

"Near the beginning of my reign."

"What tipped you off?"

"Initially, it was Master Ashir's behavior. Then, before he retired, he told me about their intentions."

"What are you going to do about selecting a new Governor?"

"You mean another consort?"

"That, too."

Bortei looked up at Minyar and smiled. Reaching up, she wound her arms around his neck. "I do love you so," she said, and kissed him passionately.

His arms went around her and he ardently kissed her back.

"Now, what did you want to talk to me about?"

"Oh, nothing. I just wanted to get rid of them."

CHAPTER SIXTEEN

Bortei was startled awake and wondered what had roused her from sleep. It must have been a thunderclap. Suddenly, flickering lightening illuminated her room. Then it was dark again. She turned on the lamp on her nightstand and looked around. Why is it so warm and humid in here, she wondered? On her nightstand, she could see a glass with juice sitting next to the lamp. She looked at it. No, what I need is a drink of water. She took the glass into the bathroom and emptied it. First rinsing it out, she filled it full of water and drank every drop of it.

Back in her bedroom, she was going to open the sliding door, but when she came close, she could hear rain and hail pelting against it.

I guess I won't open the windows tonight, she thought and stretched. "God, what time it is?" Bortei said aloud and looked at the clock. Two in the morning and not sleepy. Well, I'll go and work for a while, she thought. She rose quietly, not to waken Matyas. Like Tan Rue, his father, he always slept behind a screen next to her bedroom door.

Once in her private office, she leafed through the papers on her desk. After a time, she sat back and scratched the top of her head. It's too quiet, she thought. She missed Matya's snoring. "Let's see what's in the kitchen; I'm hungry." She went through her living room and opened the door into the hallway and ran smack into a solid stonewall.

Stunned, she braced herself against the cold stone. Bortei looked at her hands, having put them up to save her face; they were definitely going to bruise. She looked back over her shoulder; her living room looked the same as always. She rubbed her eyes with the heels of her hands and backed into the room. Her mind was blank and she could not think. An icy chill ran through her body. Her first thought was the Hidden Ones. They have abducted me!

Bortei ran across the room and yanked the sliding doors open. Rain hit her face as a cold wind blew the curtains back. The sky overhead was black with the storm. Lightning flashed across the sky and the thunder echoed. Mountains, she thought. I'm in the Aral Mountains, the hiding place of the Hidden Ones. The Oracle once told her that they had hollowed out the inside of the long mountain range near Tara, the volcano of that region.

***

Bortei awoke again to darkness, but this time she was more alert, listening. She was very tense, but didn't know why. There was no sound. Cautiously, she went to the door and slowly pulled it open. The bathroom was well lit, and before the mirror . . . she saw herself standing, dressed in her ceremonial raiment.

She quickly pulled back and silently closed the door.

Her hands flew to her face. This can't be, she thought. Bortei quickly went to the narrow slit of a window and pulled the shutters aside. She looked out over a mountainside and its bleached crags. The sky overhead was black with a few white stars showing. She was in the top part of a tower hemmed in by barren mountains.

With her mind, she reached out to the Oracle, but received no response. She felt a growing panic. Where was she and what had happened to her? And who was the lookalike in her bathroom?

She went to sit on the bed.

***

A hunched back figure slowly limped through the door. With his fingers held to his lips, he indicated for her to be quiet.

"I have come to help you," he whispered.

"I must leave here. I need to go to Azzan."

"I'm told to show you something. Something you need to know. Come, follow me."

Bortei followed him into a different room, this one dark and empty. He led her through an underground passage and out of the tower into a hollowed out chamber inside the mountain.

"Most of them have gone to a viewing room, so hopefully we won't meet anyone," her guide whispered.

They continued on into a palace fashioned on the inside of the mountain. It had a golden room and others made of crystals that were pulsating with vibrant lights. There were jeweled trees and light-filled streets; rainbows glittered in the air with a blaze of colors. The air was moist and warm.

A hand pulled at her shoulders. "Make no sound. There is danger." Ahead was a great staircase leading down and he pointed to it.

Cautiously, they descended step by step, hugging the wall. Every once in a while, her guide peered guardedly over the balustrade. They were still undetected.

Finally, they arrived at a small door cut into the stone. It opened silently. Bortei and her guide found themselves in a narrow passage that seemed to lead forever downwards. The farther down they went, the warmer the air became. Her guide motioned for her to place her hand against the wall. Even the wall was warm. She gave him a questioning look, but he only motioned for her to follow.

When he opened the next door, a blast of hot air assaulted them. Despite being inside a glass enclosure, it was hot. They walked up to the glass wall and Bortei peered over his shoulder to look into a wide and deep cave. It was shrouded in an intense, fiery red, with flickering movement reflecting off the walls.

"This is the inside of Tara," her guide explained. "The Hidden Ones use it as an energy source. The next room contains all their engines and their power sources. Come, I will show it to you on the computer." On the monitor, was the Volcano's lava conduit. The picture went downward showing the bubbling magma. It looked like a caldron from hell. It appeared to be several miles down. When the picture traveled upwards, there were a few shelves, but the conduit went straight up toward the crater.

"Here, we are several miles up. A passage was drilled into the rock to meet the conduit. The next room houses the machinery."

When they entered, Bortei expected loud engine noises, but the machines only put out a low-grade hum.

"Who looks after the machinery?" Bortei asked.

"I do."

"And why are you showing me all this?"

"Like you, I know the aim of the Hidden Ones."

"Why is it so hot and humid?" Bortei remarked.

"Because of their sensitive skin, they need the moisture."

"It makes me wonder what they look like."

"You have never seen them?"

"No."

"Don't make a sound. Step over there so you can't be seen and I will show you."

He went to a console and turned it on. On screen was a solitary individual with four arms and four hands busy adjusting dials, apparently watching a screen. He immediately sensed that he was being observed. "What is it?" he asked, and turned away from his instrument panel.

"I'm sorry to intrude. I'm on my route to check if everything is in order," Bortei's guide calmly said.

When Bortei caught sight of the individual her hand flew to her mouth to stifle a gasp. She motioned with her other hand to turn the screen off.

"Is that what they actually look like?" she whispered, barely able to contain herself.

"You think they are amusing?" her guide asked, feeling disturbed at her reaction.

"Forgive me," she said, a hint of laughter still quivering in her voice. "But they look like walruses without tusks and whiskers. Where I came from, we have animals with big dark eyes like theirs and very thick skin and no neck; except, they don't have four arms and hands. And their feet are flippers. They live in the oceans," she added. Turning serious, "Believe me, I do not take them lightly. I know the peril they present. But I was somewhat startled. After seeing Arion, I thought they would most likely look like him."

Her Hunchback guide was somewhat appeased. Checking the time, he continued, "Now, let me show you what else is going on." He went to a large screen and turned it on. At first, it flickered, then showed a view of the plaza in front of the Palace and the Temple. When he zoomed in closer, it showed a stage. Bortei's breath caught in her throat. What the close up revealed was herself in official regalia reclining on a couch.

Pointing to the screen, "Who . . . ?"

"It's a clone," her guide explained. "She is to replace you."

"And what about me?"

"You're to be killed."

"That's nice to know," Bortei quipped, suddenly at a loss for how to react. For the first time, her guide showed a glimmer of humor. "Now, what can I do to prevent it?" she asked him.

"What the Hidden Ones haven't counted on, is the Oracle. She is the only one who chooses a Queen," the Hunchback told her.

"So I was told, but what am I suppose to do?"

"Nothing. Only watch."

The screen displayed the great plaza crowded with a multitude of people. She immediately understood the meaning and gave her guide a penetrating look. The silence was great, no one stirred as the platform rose out of the ground. When the chair was empty, a sigh went up like a great wind and then a jubilant shout. They were allowed to keep their Queen. Some of her Nobles felt no love for Bortei, but she was loved by her people.

She stood in total bewilderment as the camera picked up Lord Minyar coming from the Temple accompanied by his secretary. The secretary carried a scroll in both hands.

Silence fell and the assembled multitude stood in expectation at the coming announcement. The secretary opened the scroll. His voice rang out loud and clear as he declared, "The Oracle has selected the Lord Istavan as the new adviser to the Lady Bortei and Lord Tanek as the new Governor of Atlan.

To Bortei's surprise and relief, no marriage ceremony took place. Lord Tanek simply swore fealty to the Queen. When the ceremony was over, it was high-noon and the clone bowed first to Lord Minyar and then to the people. She turned and regally mounted the stairs up to the Palace.

"Now what?" Bortei asked her guide.

"This is the Oracle's show. I was only told to bring you here and show you the Hidden Ones' power source."

Suddenly, the familiar voice in her mind said, "Alma, hold on to your hat," and she was instantly whisked directly into the private part of her bathroom.

"Where's the Clone?" she asked the Oracle.

"She has taken your place."

Bortei held her breath and just for a second, looked appalled. "I'm sorry," she said. In spite of it, she was filled with pity.

"The Clone came in here stripped of her clothes," was the last thing the Oracle told her and Bortei could feel her presence gone.

Bortei walked into the bathroom where Matyas stood in front of the door. Seconds passed as he stared at her with a fixed look. His voice was questioning when he said, "Lady Bortei?"

She only shot him a quick glance as she walked through the door.

"I'm glad this is over. What's next on the agenda?"

He gave an almost audible sigh of relief. No one, but no one could imitate the Queen. He had spotted the imposter right off and gone to Lord Minyar. Cryptically, he was told to continue as usual. "You're supposed to sup with the Lord Minyar. In about twenty minutes."

"Ah, yes. Strange day, this," Bortei only said.

***

Again they met in the neutral area of the apartment set aside for them.

When Bortei entered, Minyar rose and came toward her.

"My Lady . . ."

"Oh, knock it off," Bortei told him.

For a second he was nonplussed, then his eyes widened and there was a quick spurt of laughter. "Oh God, Bortei," he said. The relief was so overwhelming, he shook. He grabbed for her and pulled her into his arms.

"Did you expect someone else?" she joked.

"The Oracle?" he asked.

"Of course."

"But, who was . . ."

"I was told it's a Clone."

"What happened to her?"

"I was told she is to take my place." Bortei told him. "Where is she now?"

"I don't know. Let's sit down before someone comes in to serve us."

They were barely seated when a monk entered carrying a tray. Silently, he laid out the dishes and then the food. When he left, Bortei looked a Minyar, "How did you realize that she wasn't me?"

"When I met her for the first time, she seemed like a doll mimicking you, to perfection, but lacking your spontaneity and personality. There was just something amiss."

"What would you do if it were the Clone standing here?"

"Play the role. But we, I mean the monks of my order, would continue searching for you."

"Did you search for me?"

"Yes, as soon as we knew there was something wrong. Matyas swore that the individual he was dealing with wasn't you. Where have you been?"

"At the Hidden Ones' stronghold."

"And?"

"An individual said he was to show me their power plant. He knew of the Oracle and the Clone."

"Were you able to see the Hidden Ones?"

"Yes . . . they . . ." and Bortei started to laugh. "Minyar, if they weren't dangerous, they could be cute . . . maybe. Let me get some paper and I'll draw a picture." Bortei looked around. "No paper here? Well, I'll use my napkin."

After she drew the picture, she gave it to Minyar.

"You must be kidding," he exclaimed after examining her drawing.

"No, I'm not. Arion said that they are cold and emotionless and have little regard for any other life forms. They have a technology we can barely match. I think they could destroy this whole planet if they so choose. What they don't have is the material to build a spaceship. That's why they are stranded here. These are only conjectures I gathered from what Arion and Master Ashir told me."

"And why were you shown their power source."

"That was the Oracle's doing. I surmise somewhere in the future it will become important to know."

There was a knock on the door and when it opened, Minyar's secretary stood in the threshold. He gave a perfunctory bow and said, "Lord Minyar, the Lord Istavan would like to have a word with you."

"Show him in."

"He would like to have a private word with you."

"Tan Mar, tell him to come in. The Queen might be interested in what he has to say."

Tan Mar reluctantly quit the door and when he came back, he opened it all the way to allow Lord Istavan to enter.

Istavan was a man in his early fifties, tall and lean with an ascetic face. His nose was aquiline; the hair dark, graying at the temple, and it was swept off a high brow. The eyes were gray to blue. When he greeted Bortei, his voice had a fine, strong timbre. After obeisance toward the Queen, he stood tall and erect, turning a long and steady gaze on Bortei. With a short bow toward Minyar, he said in a low voice," I had hoped to have speech with you."

"What you have to say to me, you can say to her Majesty. But first of all, sit and share our meal."

Istavan made an irresolute gesture with his hand, then sat down. When Minyar looked at Bortei, she seemed to be withdrawn. He knew from their long relationship, which now spanned seventy years, that she was trying to contact the Oracle.

What Bortei heard in her head was," Alma, he's all right. I chose him. He is part human. He doesn't agree with the aims of Hidden Ones."

While she listened to the voice in her head, she watched Istavan closely from beneath her long eyelashes. When she fully looked at him, he gave her a tight smile.

"Lord Istavan," Bortei said, "I'm not the Clone. So you can talk freely to us."

There was a moment of tension that quickly passed. He smiled to cover his indecision, then inclined his head. "Lady Bortei, there is always an instance of betrayal. It only needs to be a slight, quite honest mistake, so one has to be careful."

"I understand and that is why we are here. The Hidden Ones must not suspect that their Clone has been discovered. I know you're only part human, but in accordance with us. Now, what is the intelligence you have?"

There was a short bark of laughter from Minyar. "She's always straight to the point, Lord Istavan."

"Then I will be so, also. The Hidden Ones are cloning soldiers."

"From whom do you have this information?"

"There was an error in one of their genetic productions. He was created to be an engineer, but something went wrong and he is not a . . . shall we say, perfect physical specimen . . ."

"The Hunchback," Bortei quickly injected.

"Yes. Since he maintains their machines and sees to their power stations, he can move more freely about their place."

"I see. To whom do you report?"

"There's an individual who is more like a computer than human. I'm to see him when I'm called."

"Lord Istavan, we have not met yet," Bortei told him dismissively.

***

It was a month after Prince Sinuhe's funeral when Bortei finally responded to a request for a meeting with her counselor. When she entered the small audience chamber, she met with a new face.

Lord Istavan came toward her. "Lady Bortei, may I introduce Lord Tanek."

Tanek, tall with ivory skin and silver hair, had a frosty demeanor. He looked ageless with his high-ridged, arrogant nose and a proud set to his mouth and jaw.

Tanek walked toward her. "Lady, I am here to serve you."

Before she could reply, the door opened and Lord Minyar strode in. Suddenly the air seemed to turn cold as the three men stared at each other.

"Lord Minyar, may I introduce Lord Tanek?" Istavan said and inclined his head.

"Lord Tanek," Minyar said, his face blank, betraying no emotion. He had come to lend Bortei support if needed during her first encounter with Lord Tanek.

"Lord Tanek, I hope our association will be a constructive one," Bortei said, as a chilly smile crossed her face. She knew from the Oracle that Lord Tanek, apparently human, was one of the Hidden Ones.

"It is time to install the new Governor into office." Istavan reminded her.

She raised her chin sharply. "So you have reminded me before."

At first, she and Istavan pretended to be at odds with each other, thus delaying the Governor's installation until they were sure which were plants of the Hidden Ones and which they could trust.

Her attendants were from Tan Rue's extended family. So was also her Secretary. The rest of her staff had been long in place, so she was familiar with them. The only ones they would have to watch were Lord Tanek's personnel.

"With your agreement, we think a week from now should be his official installation as the Governor of Atlan," Istavan proposed.

"That is agreeable," Bortei said. "Is there anything else on the itinerary?"

"No, that is all for now."

"Lady Bortei, may I request a private audience?" Tanek asked.

Bortei looked a Minyar and then at Istavan. When no advice was forthcoming, she inclined her head, granting the audience.

When everyone had left, Bortei turned toward Tanek. "Please be seated. What is it you wish to ask me?"

"Lady Bortei, since there was no marriage ceremony, I think there is no personal involvement required."

"It is as I understood it. By now, you should have your private affairs in order and moved in. Tomorrow, I will introduce you to the rest of my staff and you can slowly begin to acquaint yourself with the office. Is that all you wanted to ask me?"

"Yes, thank you, Lady Bortei. I will see you tomorrow."

★★★

Tanek proved to be efficient and his reports were quite to the point. Bortei was well pleased. Only Alim, one of Tan Rue's grandsons, her new secretary, complained that this didn't give him enough to do.

The first difference of opinion between herself and Tanek came during the appointment of a new Supreme Judge. There were two candidates. The one Tanek proposed was well-versed in the law and had an impressive record, but when Bortei interviewed him, he seemed too rigid in his demeanor and interpretation of the law.

When Tanek inquired of the reason she rejected his choice, she explained, "Yes, he is amply qualified. His credentials are impeccable. But to be a judge, one has to have an understanding and a feel for human nature. There is the letter of the law, and there is the spirit of the law. Many injustices have been committed by strictly adhering to the letter of the law. Human behavior is never cut and dry."

He had given her a long inscrutable look, then slowly turned to walk out of her office.

She wondered, and not for the first time, how to keep this precarious balance of interacting with someone she knew to be a ruthless enemy. She had watched him stretching out tentative feelers, trying to comprehend what was for him an alien society. Since there was no intimate interaction with him, she seldom saw him outside official meetings.

CHAPTER SEVENTEEN

When Anahita came into the Crystal room, as always he had to stop; this was all his and he had almost lost it, and probably would have lost his life. When he thought of it, his hatred for the Atlantes rose like bitter bile. Although the incident had been a long time ago when Anahita was very young, it still enraged him. He had been at a beach, supposedly guarding four young Iasis and three young women. The young ones had been playing in the ocean. But instead of standing guard, he had been horsing around with the women, trying to induce them to respond to his amorous intentions. His blood had been running high and his hormones clouding his senses. Anahita's whole mind was focused on his arousal. He had finally caught one of them, but only because she stumbled and fell. She fought him, but it only heightened his excitement. Then the other two cuddled up beside him. Only after he lay panting in the sand, did he become aware of the cries for help. He had carefully crawled up on the dune to see three ships. As Anahita watched, a full load of fish was being dumped into the middle ship. What had made his blood run cold was the four Iasi children clinging to the net, terrified and screaming for help. There had been nothing he could do.

Anahita had had to throw himself on top of one of the woman, yelling for the others to stay hidden behind the dune. He had run for his field glasses while one the women snatched up the communicator. She had demanded that he called the warriors, but instead, he had called Mardos, his half-brother. After explaining the situation, he had told Mardos to bring explosives. What Anahita hadn't counted on was that the fishermen, after dumping their catch, were processing the fish right there. One of the men had taken one of the children, and thinking that he had found a new food source, chopped its head off. The fisherman had yelled out when a spurt of blood hit him in the face. The color of the blood had been blue. The Atlantes' blood is red; but the blood of the Iasi is blue. Thinking about it in retrospect, it occurred to Anahita . . . that had been what saved the other children. The men had been shocked by the blue color of the blood.

After nightfall, Anahita and Mardos had swum out to the ships. When Anahita had looked over the railing, he saw that the young Iasis were locked in a cage. To kill his boredom, the sentry kicked at it every time he passed. Mardos eased himself over the railing and crept up behind the sentry, then killed him. He freed the children and told them to swim to the beach. After they had safely exited the water, Anahita and Mardos had placed the explosives against the side of the ships. When they were back on the beach; Mardos had triggered the explosives.

Now Anahita and the women had to get their story straight. All young females belonged to the dominant male. To infringe on his rights could mean a fight to the death. Anahita was not ready to enter in a battle he knew he could not win. Their story had to be simple and believable. Ashita told the head of their clan that Anahita and she were readying food for the picnic and that Minory was standing watch. She explained how Minory had slipped and tumbled down the dune. They had had to dig her out and were trying to clean the sand from her mouth and nose when they heard the children screaming for help. They realized that there was nothing they could do. So they had to watch helplessly as one of the Little Ones was killed. Anahita had called Mardos to bring explosives and when it became dark they swam out and rescued the children, then blew up the ships. The story was simple and plausible and Anahita and the three women adhered to it. After some consideration, they were believed. A mishap to the dominant male brought Anahita to the forefront. After battling several contenders, he had come out as the winner, and now he reveled in the knowledge that he was the dominant male with all the privileges.

He was startled out of his reminiscence when his half-brother Mardos suddenly entered the room. He hoped that he would bring new updates on the Queen's progress. He had waited a long time to get even with the Atlantes for the nightmares they had caused him.

***

Tanek was called to a meeting with Mardos the Iasi. The Iasi never knew that they were called the Hidden Ones. Mardos was the right-hand man and half-brother to Anahita, the Iasi's tyrant who coveted to rule Atlan.

Tanek walked down a corridor that led deep inside the hollowed out mountain. He passed the prism that reflected the light shining from above, thus illuminating the cavern. He came to a small door cut into the stone. It opened silently and Tanek stepped into a narrowed passage that led downward. Tanek knew he was now inside Tara, the Volcano. Arion had brought no reports of progress.

So he was walking a tightrope; there were too many undercurrents he was not yet able to figure out.

The Queen, who was supposed to be a clone, did not follow the laid out directives. Her behavior had become enigmatic and he could not discern her intensions since there was supposed to be only interaction at the business meetings. Anahita was getting impatient, even though there was progress. The Atlantes have become more educated, and their technical knowledge was nearing the desired level.

When the door slowly opened, Tanek moved to face Mardos.

"My Lord," Tanek bowed to him.

"Tanek, please dispense with the rituals. I am here. Maybe I'm putting my head in the noose, but I need to put out my feelers to see if you can assist me."

"What can I help you with?"

"Ashita came to me. She is worried about Anahita. He is behaving strangely. The incident on the beach where we lost the little boy is still preying on his mind. It is not so much the death of the child, but the peril it almost put him in. She thinks he is talking himself into a mental breakdown. He is muttering about getting even with the Atlantes. Then, there is a rumor that people with certain qualifications have disappeared; people with technical know-how. Have you heard anything about it?"

Tanek was taken aback for a moment. Mardos broke into his silence and said. "Tanek, we have to trust each other, maybe with our lives. You know I am Anahita's half-brother, and I too have noticed his behavior becoming erratic. There is something going on, but I can't put my finger on it. Also, Manolo is shedding more and more his detached attitude. He has repeatedly averred that he is only interested in science, in genetic engineering. But I have always suspected that all this is a pose. He is very much on top of what's going on, and he is getting tired of Anahita's irrational behavior."

"Is Manolo presenting a danger?"

"He may be an unknown threat, adding to this intrigue," Mardos informed him.

Tanek took a deep breath. "Will you keep on top of it, for the sake of Atlan? Also, the people disappearing with the technical know-how have been kidnapped and sent to the Island we came to when we first landed on Atlan. The shuttle is still there and these people are being used to make it operational."

Mardos looked stunned.

Suddenly the door opened and the nameless Hunchback came noiselessly into the room. "My Lords," he said, "I have the answer to your riddle."

"What is it?" Mardos asked.

"The Lord Anahita plans to leave Atlan in the shuttle."

"But where would he go? The shuttle holds no more than thirty individuals."

"My Lord Mardos, he has prepared a list of those who would go with him. Your name is not on it, nor Ashita's."

"How do you know all this?"

"As my Lords know, I tend the machinery. Sometimes Lord Anahita asks if this or that is feasible. What I have deduced from his questions is that he wants to create a giant tsunami. He wants to drown all the Atlantes after he lifts off from Atlan."

"But that's insane!" Mardos exclaimed. "What's going to happen to the rest of us?"

"He is not concerned with anyone left behind. He will only take women and children.

Mardos and Tanek looked at each other in total shock.

"You need to inform the Queen," the Hunchback told them.

"I hate to dissolution you. The Queen is a clone."

"Yes, I know, Lord Mardos. She attends only the social functions, and she moves only under the direction of the Queen. The Lady Bortei is still in the picture."

"How do you know?"

"Lord Mardos, I am in contact with the real Queen. She has asked me to be on standby. She will have a job for me to do."

"Do you know what it is?"

"No, Lord Mardos. She hasn't told me yet."

"Will you keep us informed?"

"Yes, I do this with the Queen's permission."

***

"Alma." The whisper came in the dark chamber. When Bortei raised herself up on her bed, the voice continued. "Alma, get dressed."

"What's going on?" Bortei asked.

"You need to take a trip." Bortei could hear amusement in the Oracle's voice.

When the door crept silently open, Bortei spun around. It was the Hunchback.

He whispered, "Lady, the Oracle has asked me to bring you these clothes and a layout of the inside of the volcano."

Bortei inspected the clothes and looked in surprise at the Hunchback. "Strange looking clothes; how do you put them on?"

There was an amused chuckle. "Alma, put them on the floor and it will explain itself."

She laid the clothes out. "Is this where the legs go in?" pointing to the pants.

"Yes, and don't put them on backwards. Look at his getup."

"You got a name?" Bortei asked.

"Yes, my Lady. My name is Ossa."

"All right, Ossa now help me put these garments on the right way." When she was dressed, she said, "They feel very comfortable," and looked at herself in the mirror. "And now what?"

"Now Ossa will do a job he was assigned to do, and you will take a trip. You will meet a woman who will help you to save Atlan. Anahita is planning to destroy Atlan. He has gathered enough explosives to break up an island and to create a huge tsunami that he hopes will sweep over the whole continent of Atlan. Mardos, Anahita's half-brother, and Tanek will do all they can to save the population of Atlan. And Alma, take those plans with you and hang on to your hat."

Chapter Eighteen

It was a warm sunny day and Bortei found herself walking down a crowded avenue. The people strolling down the street were looking happy and alive, talking and laughing. They seem to be having a good time, Bortei thought as she changed the rolled up plans she was carrying over to her other arm. But looking around, it all felt strange. Where in the world am I? What's going on? she thought to the Oracle.

"Keep on walking," Bortei was told.

All right, Bortei thought. At least in this getup, I don't look out of place. She came to a plaza where there were tables and chairs outdoors. People were dining, some just drinking. Looks interesting, Bortei thought. I think I will sit down and have something. Aw, I don't have any money. Well, a good idea gone south. Suddenly a woman with the most incredible green eyes walked up to her and asked, "Are you Bortei?"

"Yes, my name is Bortei," she answered and looked a little suspiciously at her.

"Language translator," she enlightened her. "And are you the Queen of Atlan?"

"Yes, to that, too."

"Well, I thought I was going nuts when a voice in my head told me to come here and meet the Queen of Atlan."

Bortei started to laugh and the woman with the green eyes chimed in. "Do you know who the voice in your head was?"

"No, but she was very insistent that I come here. By the way, my name is Sabrina.

"I am glad to meet you, Sabrina. Can we go somewhere to sit?"

"How about that outdoor café you just passed?"

Bortei grimaced. "I don't have any money that would be accepted there."

"That's okay, I have some."

When they were seated, Bortei placed the very intriguing roll that were likely some kind of blueprints on the table. Sabrina looked at the roll, and raised an eyebrow.

"Let's look at them, later," Bortei suggested.

"Sabrina ordered iced coffee. When Bortei gave her a dubious look, she encouraged her. "Try it; you'll like it." Bortei took a sip and immediately agreed with Sabrina.

After they emptied the goblets, Sabrina said, "Now, tell me what am I supposed to help you with?"

"The Oracle didn't tell you?"

"No, she was very mysterious. She intrigued me."

"Well, it can't be told in a nutshell. It's a long story and a very convoluted one. There is an alien called Anahita, and he is threatening to destroy Atlan."

"Well, that sounds questionable. How does he envision doing that?"

"By using explosives to blow up an atoll and create a tsunami massive enough to engulf a major part of Atlan, if not all of it."

Sabrina's expression was dubious. "Can you not apprehend this individual?"

"Anahita's people are called Iasi. They created a city within a hollowed out mountain that includes a volcano they use as an energy source. They are very technologically advanced and are supposed to be super intelligent, except for Anahita, who seems to have become unhinged. His own people have become leery of him and are aiding me by negating his scheme. Also, his people are very reclusive. I think very few people have seen one. They mostly act through intermediaries, and most of them are genetically engineered. The present Queen is a clone. Anahita thinks I am dead and this clone has taken my place. Naturally, she operates under my direction. I also have supporters among the Iasi aiding me."

"Let's unroll those plans you have," Sabrina told her. Sabrina took a long time studying the layout. "Do you know what you have here?" Sabrina asked Bortei.

"No. I guess this is where you come in."

"This layout shows the whole installation of the Iasi. It shows where they live, and the equipment for the environmental control. It's also a layout of the power grid. It outlines their whole life support and that they are very sophisticated. They have extensive technological knowledge. What do you think your Oracle wants us to do with all of this?"

"I don't know. What I think is, that if we go to my home world, we may have a better idea. How am I going to get home?"

"That's no problem," Sabrina told her with a toothy grin. "Have you ever been on a spaceship?"

"No. What's that?"

"I think showing you is better than talking about it. So, now I should call an air-car to fly us out to the spaceport."

"I don't know if I'm going to like all these new experiences," Bortei quipped.

"You'll get over it," Sabrina promised her.

***

Sabrina's Spitfire took Bortei's breath away. "What do you do with this?" she asked.

"You go inside and relax. That's how you will get home. Let's go inside."

Both walked to the controls and Sabrina told Bortei to sit in the co-pilot's seat. Then Sabrina went through preflight checks and found that the coordinates for Bortei's home world were already laid in. She called the tower for permission to lift off. When the ship came to life, it lifted into the air, causing a shocked expression on Bortei's face. "God in heaven, what's next?" she exclaimed.

"Alma, have her show you how to fly this ship."

When Bortei looked at Sabrina, Sabrina said, "Tall order."

"You heard her?" Bortei asked.

"Yes, I have a few abilities in that direction. I wonder why she wants you to learn how to fly this ship. You have no idea what she has in mind?"

"No. I have trusted her all these years. I guess I have to believe she knows what she is talking about."

"Okay, let's begin by giving you a rudimentary understanding of how this ship works."

"How long will it take for me to get home?" she asked Sabrina after they had been in space for seven days.

"In no time. I think you have a feel for Spitfire now."

"I'm not that confident."

"I want you to listen to me very closely. When you hear a bell chime, close your eyes tightly. When the bell chimes twice, you can open them again. Don't open your eyes until you hear the bell twice. Now close them, tight."

After the second chime, Sabrina told Bortei to look out of the window."

"Wow, what's that?"

"Your home world."

"Looks like a ball in space."

Sabrina laughed. "I guess you have never seen your world from up here. Now, tell me, where do you want me to put you down?"

"What do you mean?"

"Sabrina, use the coordinates I put into your computer," the Oracle told her.

"Well, that will make it easy. Bortei, see those pads? Stand on them and don't move."

After Bortei materialized into an empty room, Sabrina parked Spitfire on one of the Moons and then appeared behind Bortei, saying, "That wasn't too bad."

Bortei screamed as she spun around. When she saw it was only Sabrina, she said, "What are you trying to do, give me a heart attack? How did you get in here?"

Suddenly the door flew open and two guards burst in. Bortei let out a long sigh. "I'm all right. This is a friend of mine. Thanks for responding so promptly."

The guards left reluctantly, still keeping an eye on Sabrina. When the door closed behind them, Bortei turned on Sabrina with a jaundiced eye. "How did you do that?" she demanded.

"Something I can do. I can appear and disappear. It's a long story."

Both spun around when the door opened again. Minyar and Tanek stood at the threshold. "Lady Bortei?" the Lord Minyar asked.

"Yes, I'm the real article," Bortei answered. Then their eyes fell on Sabrina. "A friend of mine, and the Oracle's," Bortei quipped.

"Sorry, sirs," Sabrina said, giving Bortei a sidelong glance. I'm Sabrina Hennesee. The Oracle contacted me to help your Queen. I don't know in what capacity, but she will let me know, I hope."

"A guard alerted us, saying he heard voices in this room. Where did you come from?" Minyar asked.

"What's going on?" Bortei asked, ignoring Minyar's question.

"Manolo killed Anahita, and I think you're in danger," Tanek told her.

"Who is Manolo?" Bortei asked.

"He was the power behind Anahita. Anahita was only his puppet. Only very recently did we put two and two together. I think you know about the cloned soldiers?"

"Yes, what about them?"

"Manolo had them round up the people and then set all the cities on fire."

"He did what? Why would he do such a thing?"

"His plan is to enslave the people. People without property, without a home or money and nowhere to go. The cloned soldiers have built barracks in the Calahari desert. I think that's where they are herding the people."

"Tanek, Minyar, what are we going to do about it?" Bortei asked. "Do you have a plan of action?"

"No, not yet; we just discovered it," Tanek told her.

"Sabrina, any ideas?"

"No, we need more information to plan any action."

Suddenly the door burst open and the Hunchback almost tumbled through. When he saw Bortei, he pointed a finger at her, croaking, "You're still alive, you're alive," and nearly fainted.

Bortei went over to him and bent down, asking, "Ossa, what's going on?"

He exhaled a big sigh of relief. "You are Bortei. Oh god, thank god."

Bortei helped him to rise from the floor. "Ossa, what has happened? Speak to me."

"Manolo killed the clone. I thought it was you. Thank god, you're alive."

"Why would he kill the clone?" Tanek asked him.

"So he can take over Atlan. This has always been his plan. There's going to be a big celebration. Atlan will at last belong to the Iasi," so his rhetoric went. "I don't know how many of the Iasi will go along with him."

"I will get Spitfire and we can fly out to that desert and see what's going on. I think it would be a good idea to talk to the people first and see what the situation is before we take any action," Sabrina told Bortei.

"I think you're right. That will be the best way to handle this situation. What's a Spitfire?" Tanek asked.

"I will let Bortei explain it to you," Sabrina told Tanek. Turning to Bortei, "You and company go up on the Palace roof. I will pick you up from there." As soon as Sabrina was out in the hall, she disappeared and materialized on Spitfire.

When she appeared over Atlan, she locked onto the people on the roof of the Palace and beamed them up.

"Interesting way of travel you have here," Minyar told her while he looked around the ship. When he looked at

Sabrina's toothy grin, he quipped, "I suspect you will let Bortei explain that, too."

"It would take too long, and time is short."

"All right, Sabrina, now what?"

"My Lord Tanek, I will fly you out to the desert and we can go from there."

Suddenly there was a flash of light and the Hunchback materialized on Spitfire.

"Oh, my goodness, wonders never cease." Bortei exclaimed, but was not as shocked as the others. "The Oracle?" she asked him.

"Yes, Your Majesty. She wants me to tell you that all the Iasi are dead and that she had me place explosives around their installation."

There was a stunned silence. "How did they die?" Lord Tanek asked him.

"The Oracle asked me to funnel the volcanic gases into their inhabited areas. They are all dead now." Ossa shuddered. "It was horrible, all those dead bodies."

"We are over the encampment," Sabrina's voice broke into the silence.

There was something like a thunderclap and the Oracle's voice said, "Beam Lord Tanek and Lord Minyar down to the camp."

When they had materialized at the camp, the Oracle continued. "Sabrina, go home in your special way and take Ossa home with you. Sorry, but I need Spitfire to destroy the Iasi's installation. So, go now."

When Sabrina started to protest, she received a light electric shock to her forehead.

"Please Sabrina, it is necessary."

"Okay, Ossa, hold onto your hat," Sabrina told him, and taking him by the hand, disappeared.

"Now to you, Alma. You are the last Queen of Atlan. You have helped defeat the Iasi's intentions to rule Atlan. Their tyranny would have been something no one should suffer. Now, take the pilot's seat and turn the ship toward Tara and finish this job."

"What do you want me to do?" Bortei asked.

"Do just as I tell you. When we reach the Volcano, I will take over. So trust me just a little longer."

When they closed in on the Volcano, Bortei felt her mind being prompted by the Oracle. "Close your eyes," she was told. "Be calm and look within. I am with you and we will meet each other, at last. You need only trust that your job here is finished and there is another place for you."

Suddenly Bortei felt the violent vibration of the ship and could hear the roar of the engines. There were impact noises as the photons hit places inside the Volcano. Then Bortei and the Oracle flew Spitfire into the Volcano and it exploded.

***

After a period of time, Lord Tanek and Lord Minyar returned to Azzan, but it was gone. They could not believe the devastation. The volcano had exploded, sending down rocks and boulders. The city now lay buried under cinders, ashes and lava. Tara's cone had collapsed, and the height of Tara had changed with the eruption.

The Iasi had run a power plant using volcanic steam. They had created a world by carving out grottos and a palace into the stone. They could have been a positive force, but chose to be destructive.

Tanek and Minyar turned away, slowly retracing their steps. There was nothing there.

"Why did the Oracle have all the Iasi killed?" Minyar suddenly asked.

"Because she discerned that they were a danger to the Atlantes. The Iasi never regarded them as more than things for their personal use and gain. They considered them working animals, maybe even as a food source."

Minyar looked askance. "But that's . . . that . . . I have no word for that. They must have realized that we were sentient."

"Yes, but not on their level. If you remember, the fishermen saw the Iasi children as a food source."

Minyar began thinking aloud, "With no survivors, the Oracle could destroy Tara and the whole mountain range. I think she also must have discerned that the Atlantes and the Iasi would never have reconciled their differences and in the end may have annihilated each other."

Minyar and Tanek walked for a while in brooding silence. Then Minyar asked Tanek, "What does an ex-High Priest, and an ex-Governor do now?"

"We could continue what Bortei started. Build a better and more equitable society, and prevent power ever to be held in the hand of one individual."

"She was a remarkable woman."

"Amen to that," Minyar agreed.